Kitty glanced ~~at her~~
watch and Se~~rena felt a touch~~
of panic. It u~~as a relief to have~~
something to ~~focus on besides the~~
work with him. He didn't trust
this sudden attraction. He
needed to test this feeling. Give it
time. Get to know her.

"On second thought, it isn't a housekeeper I need. It's more of a household manager."

"Not someone to scrub the bathrooms and cook your meals? I warn you, I'm not great at housework."

"No," he said dismissively. "A person who could oversee what needs to be done, find the people to do it."

She crinkled up her nose in a way he found delightful. "And you seriously think that person could be me?"

"You've proved yourself to be formidably organized and efficient."

"But I know absolutely nothing about your needs."

"My needs?"

Needs of a kind that had nothing to do with furniture or wallpaper and everything to do with this lovely woman came immediately to mind. The sudden flush high on her cheekbones made him aware her thoughts might have followed a similar path.

Dear Reader,

People often ask me if I have a favorite among the heroes and heroines I've written. It's like asking a mother who her favorite child is! I couldn't possibly choose; I love each of them. After all, I spend a lot of time with my characters and find myself missing them after I type "The End."

None more so than Kitty and Sebastian in *Second Chance with His Cinderella*. In spite of the betrayal and heartbreak she's suffered in her past, Kitty is warm, kind and fun. To gorgeous, brooding Sebastian Delfont, she is a ray of sunshine in what he feels, despite his wealth and privilege, to be a life defined by loss.

The attraction between them is instant and powerful—but there are barriers stemming from their past traumas and disappointments on which they stumble before reaching the happily-ever-after they so richly deserve.

The setting for Kitty and Sebastian's love story is a wonderful old house that Sebastian has inherited in one of the most prestigious areas of London, which helps bring them together.

I hope you enjoy Kitty and Sebastian's journey to realizing they are each other's once-in-a-lifetime love.

Warm regards,

Kandy

Second Chance with His Cinderella

Kandy Shepherd

HARLEQUIN®

Romance™

Recycling programs
for this product may
not exist in your area.

ISBN-13: 978-1-335-40700-9

Second Chance with His Cinderella

Copyright © 2022 by Kandy Shepherd

All rights reserved. No part of this book may be used or reproduced in
any manner whatsoever without written permission except in the case of
brief quotations embodied in critical articles and reviews.

This is a work of fiction. Names, characters, places and incidents
are either the product of the author's imagination or are used fictitiously.
Any resemblance to actual persons, living or dead, businesses,
companies, events or locales is entirely coincidental.

This edition published by arrangement with Harlequin Books S.A.

For questions and comments about the quality of this book,
please contact us at CustomerService@Harlequin.com.

Harlequin Enterprises ULC
22 Adelaide St. West, 41st Floor
Toronto, Ontario M5H 4E3, Canada
www.Harlequin.com

Printed in U.S.A.

Kandy Shepherd swapped a career as a magazine editor for a life writing romance. She lives on a small farm in the Blue Mountains near Sydney, Australia, with her husband, daughter and lots of pets. She believes in love at first sight and real-life romance—they worked for her! Kandy loves to hear from her readers. Visit her at kandyshepherd.com.

To Julie O'Loughlin and Lynne Bartlett, who so expertly and cheerfully packed up my possessions for me when I moved house—and gave me insight and inspiration for this story.

Praise for
Kandy Shepherd

CHAPTER ONE

SEBASTIAN DELFONT STOOD still and silent on the balcony of his Docklands penthouse as he gazed for the last time at the early-morning mist rising from the Thames and shrouding his view of the London skyline. His fists curled over the top of the cold metal railing so tightly it hurt him. But he scarcely noticed. He could no longer evade his duty to the name he bore. He had to leave here and say goodbye to his independence, his freedom to live his life on his terms. Death had swept through his family and now it was his time to step up.

He heaved a deep profound sigh, knowing there was no one nearby to hear him. How could he possibly feel sorry for himself? Immense wealth. Privilege. A place in the highest echelons of society. All came with the inheritance. Yet the family history was scarred by tragedy and loss. He felt trapped by that story. But he could not walk away from it. He was a Delfont and with that came responsibility and duty, no matter how unwelcome.

The women he'd engaged to pack up the apartment would soon be here. PWP had come highly recommended as specialist packers giving discretion, skill and care. He could only have the best professionals handling his possessions. Of his books, artworks and collectibles some were valuable, others valuable only to him. All were important. In some way they cocooned him with the security he had longed for while growing up. Many of the items would have to go into storage as they wouldn't suit the period house on Cheyne Walk. Like he himself didn't suit, had never suited.

Once the packers arrived, his home here would be dismantled until it would no longer be his own; he had already let it for a hefty rent. He could only ever regard the house he was moving to as his grandfather's, no matter what the deeds of ownership might say. And he had never spent a happy moment there.

It was shaping up to be a typical October day in London, unable to make up its mind whether to be crisp and autumnal or cloudy and drizzly. As Sebastian started to turn and go back inside, a shaft of sunlight pierced the grey clouds. He watched for a long moment as its brilliance illuminated the sky and the water below. His Spanish mother had been superstitious, and a part of him could not help hoping that this was an omen for the times to come.

* * *

Kitty Clements never felt nervous at the start of a new assignment. Why would she? Launching their company PWP—People Who Pack—two years ago with her friend Claudia had been an excellent way for her to make a new start. Packing prized possessions for clients moving house was straightforward, interesting—who could resist a peek into other people's lives?—and gave her the under-the-radar anonymity she craved.

But today her hand wasn't quite steady as she keyed in the code to admit her to the private elevator that would shoot her up to the ninth floor and the Docklands penthouse that their client, Sebastian Delfont, was vacating. She'd been warned the client might be 'difficult' and she wasn't quite sure what that could mean. She had cause to distrust difficult men. But this was a client. And the job was the most lucrative they'd contracted in their two years of business. Everything here had to go without a hitch. Their business relied heavily on recommendation and word of mouth. Who knew where a testimonial from a wealthy client like Sebastian Delfont could lead?

The elevator deposited her in the starkly elegant marble foyer of the penthouse. Her nervousness dissipated at the reassuring sight of folded flat packing boxes propped against a wall, along with bales of wrapping paper and boxes of sealing tape that had been delivered the evening before by a member of their team. The tools of her new trade. She would find more placed in each of the rooms. This was a substantial job and she and Claudia would be here for several days. As soon as she was inside, she would put in her earbuds, switch on some get-those-boxes-packed music and get going. She knew what she was doing. There was nothing to worry about.

As the double doors to the penthouse opened Kitty looked up. She caught her breath. *Difficult* wasn't the thought that came to mind at her first sight of Sebastian Delfont. *Outrageously handsome* was more to the point. And young, thirtyish she guessed. Why hadn't Claudia told her? Claudia was the one who did the initial negotiating with clients; surely she hadn't failed to notice he was hot, if a touch forbidding? *Hotter than hot.*

Tall, broad-shouldered, with black hair that looked as if it was past time for a cut and a lean, chiselled face with more than a morning's dark stubble, he was dressed in black jeans and black turtleneck sweater that made no secret of a strong athletic body. Not that she should be noticing. *How could she not notice?*

'Mr D… Delfont,' she managed to stammer out. 'Kitty Clements from PWP.'

Dark brows furrowed. 'I was expecting Claudia.' His voice was deep, resonant and very posh.

Kitty felt a quick flash of the self-doubt she still battled to overcome. Of course he would be disappointed. Claudia was tall, red-haired, glamorous in her own understated way. Kitty was shorter and curvier, more cute than couture. Not, perhaps, to be taken as seriously as her friend. How had that horrid red-top tabloid headlined her? *Pretty, Plump and Predatory.* She shuddered at the very thought of it. The man who'd lost her a promising career in public relations had been the predator, not her. But no one had believed her.

She forced a bright professional smile. 'Claudia is caught up in traffic; a lorry overturned on the motorway. She'll be here as soon as she can. In the meantime, I'm ready to start packing if you'd like to point me in the right direction.'

'I'll show you exactly what I require,' he said.

'Of course,' she said. It wasn't in her nature to be subservient but in this business the client's needs ruled.

Kitty followed him into the apartment, taking care to keep a good distance apart. She couldn't help a heartfelt silent 'wow'. PWP had packed up flats, suburban houses, country manor houses, even a houseboat. But nothing as spectacular as this. The enormous apartment was all stainless steel and glass and stark designer furniture. She looked through walls of glass doors to a spectacular view of the Thames.

'Very impressive,' she said.

'Yes, it is,' he said. 'I'll be sorry to leave here.'

I would be too, she almost said. But her own

feelings and thoughts didn't come into this job. Sometimes clients didn't even bother to remember her name. And that anonymity suited her very well.

Kitty knew this client was moving to an even more impressive house on Cheyne Walk, Chelsea, one of the most prestigious and expensive addresses in London. PWP had been employed to unpack there. But it was not her place to chit-chat about his move. She was just here to pack up what her grandfather called 'goods and chattels' as quickly and safely as possible. It was PWP policy that packers didn't get personal with clients.

Sebastian Delfont picked up a small black digital camera from the console and handed it to her. 'Before you start to pack, I want you to photograph everything so it can be placed in exactly the same way in the new house. The library is particularly important.'

It was an unusual request, but nothing she couldn't handle. 'I can do that,' she said.

'I'll take you to the library first,' he said.

Kitty followed him through the living areas and past the kitchen. The rooms were all furnished in the same modern style, shades of grey and metallics a foil for a collection of contemporary paintings and sculptures. It was very masculine. Was there a Mrs Delfont? There was certainly no feminine touch here.

The library was a surprise; it was lined with

bookshelves crammed with books from top to bottom. The limited wall space was covered in brightly coloured paintings that jarred with the sombre tones of the rest of the apartment. Claudia had warned her there'd be a lot of books. They'd had to order more of the smaller book boxes than ever before. Paper was heavy and a bigger box packed with books would be too heavy to handle, both for the packer and the mover who would transport them. Thankfully, there was a library ladder that would help her access the top levels. Still, it was a daunting task.

'That's a lot of books,' she said. 'I'd better get started.'

Her client put up his hand in a halt sign. A masculine hand yet somehow elegant, long fingers with well-kept nails. The man had the looks to be an actor or a model. But she had never heard of him. And that accent didn't come from lessons at drama school.

'Not just yet,' he said. 'First, I want you to photograph each row of books. They have to be placed in exactly the same order on the bookshelves in the other house. There mustn't be one book out of place.'

Kitty swallowed hard. So this was what Claudia meant by saying their client might be difficult. Obsessive, it seemed. Would he be standing over her shoulder, directing her every move? She gritted her teeth at the thought. But that was okay.

He was the client. His demands were nothing she couldn't handle, although she would have to tread carefully. As long as he didn't get too physically close to her. She couldn't deal with that.

'I understand,' she said very seriously. 'I think I might also record the order of the rows in a note-book as an extra working document and then label each box with a code.'

'Good,' he said as he nodded. And she saw what she could only interpret as a flash of gratitude in his slate-grey eyes.

Sebastian went to turn on his heel to leave the room but then paused, arrested by the way Kitty Clements's hair, loosely tied behind her head, glowed golden in that sole shaft of sunlight that filtered through the window.

She was very pretty. He fought for a less clichéd word to describe her. Blonde hair, a heart-shaped face, blue eyes—what else could he think but pretty? Pretty, cute, curvaceous. They all worked. Her black leggings and a long baggy black T-shirt with a bright pink PWP logo emblazoned across her chest did nothing to hide her shape.

But it was more than her pretty face and shapely figure that made him look twice. He'd seen warmth and kindness in those blue eyes, understanding without condescension. She hadn't questioned his requests, just thoughtfully suggested further ways of making sure she did what he needed. His doctor had reassured him he did not have obsessive compulsive disorder, but he knew his desire for control over certain aspects of his personal environment wasn't everyday behaviour and it sometimes made people uncomfortable around him.

Not, so it seemed, Kitty Clements. After all he'd been through with Lavinia, his former fiancée, who had fought to turn him into what she wanted and ruthlessly mocked his need for orderliness in his library, he was grateful for Kitty's quiet understanding. Even though she was just a woman he had engaged to pack up his possessions.

He knew he should leave the library and let her get on with it—after all, he was paying her by the hour—but he found himself compelled to stay.

'What made you go into packing as a job?' he asked. The PWP website had listed both her and her business partner Claudia Eaton as directors.

'I wanted to be my own boss.'

'Understandable. Why packing?' He noticed how sleekly muscled Kitty's arms were; her workday was probably equivalent to a weightlifting session at a gym.

'I had to pack up my flat in a hurry, had no time to pack for myself and wasn't in the slightest bit happy with the way the movers did it.'

No explanation of why she'd had to pack up in such a hurry. Sebastian felt he was on the receiving end of a practised spiel she no doubt gave to any client who showed interest. It did nothing to deflect his interest; rather it made him intrigued about what story lay behind those guileless blue eyes.

'I see,' he said.

'Claudia had a similar experience. We knew we could do better. Much better. At first we worked freelance with a big removals company then set up on our own. We found there was a demand for women packers. People believe we take more care with their possessions, and some people feel more comfortable with women in their house.' Her smile was like a practised punctuation to her story. Yet it lit her eyes and seemed to up the wattage of the sunbeam that danced through her hair.

'Why PWP?' he asked. The small specialist company had come highly recommended for honesty and discretion.

'People Who Pack,' she said. 'We started with Ladies Who Pack. After all, our earlier clients referred to us as "those ladies who pack".' Her smile dimmed and she gave a small, almost imperceptible shudder. 'But it brought us the wrong kind of attention. We were also accused of being discriminatory. So we amended the name and went from there. It keeps us fit and we enjoy it. Now we have a team of women working for us.'

She looked pointedly at her watch. 'And, talking of working, I have a lot of books to pack.'

'And you want me out of here,' he said.

'Please. I know what I have to do, and I don't need you to direct me. I'll call you if I need any clarification.' Her words were lightly said and delivered with another smile, but it was a definite dismissal.

To his surprise, Sebastian was okay with that. He felt reassured his books would be packed—and unpacked—just the way he wanted them to be. His spirits—subdued since he'd awoken this morning, aware that it was the last day of his life as a lone wolf—lifted with the knowledge. There could be no doubt he was in good hands with PWP—and Kitty Clements.

'I'll leave you to it,' he said as he somewhat reluctantly left the room.

Kitty was fascinated by the contents of Sebastian's bookshelves. The titles ranged from leather-bound first editions and histories of London to the latest bestsellers. She had to force herself not to get too distracted by them. She was here to pack, not to browse. While the books were mainly in English, there were titles in Spanish too. Surprisingly, there was an entire row of paperback romances all by one author, Marisol Matthew. Kitty held a title in her hand for a moment too long before she carefully placed it in the box with the others—in strict order of publication. Memories came flooding back.

After her parents had died when she was fourteen years old, Kitty had been brought up by her maternal grandparents. Her beloved grandmother had been an avid reader of romance novels and Marisol Matthew one of her favourite authors. Towards the end of her battle with cancer, Gran had become too weak to read or hold a book. The last story Kitty had read out loud to her, as she'd sat by her bedside, was by Marisol Matthew—a rousing tale with a gorgeous Spanish hero. Gran had loved it.

Sebastian Delfont didn't seem to be the type to be a romance reader, but she had learned the hard way not to judge people by appearances. There was also a shelf packed with the latest thrillers. One thing was for sure, she wouldn't ask him. Part of the PWP code of conduct was to keep up the illusion of privacy by never commenting on the client's belongings. No matter the sometimes startling and strange things they might come across.

Kitty was well into the rhythm of packing books, taking notes and coding boxes when Claudia arrived. Her best friend and business partner rushed to her side.

'I'm so sorry to leave you alone with a new client, a man. But it couldn't be helped. The fuel tanker blocking the way was in danger of exploding. We actually had to turn around and go back on the wrong side of the road until we could get onto a diversion. Are you okay?'

Kitty brushed aside her friend's apologies.

Claudia had been there for her through the entire unpleasant time she'd reported the director of the big public relations firm where she'd worked for attempted sexual assault. She hadn't been believed and the incident had been turned against her.

'I'm fine. Seriously. Sebastian Delfont is okay. I feel safe with him.'

'Good. I liked him too. Although I thought he might be difficult about the way he wanted things packed.'

Kitty shook her head. 'He's exacting. But not difficult. Nothing we can't handle.'

'I'm glad to hear that.'

Kitty turned to her friend. 'But you might have warned me about how good-looking he is. We've never packed for such a hot client. It's quite distracting. I... I didn't know where to look at first.'

Claudia smirked. 'Does it matter? As you haven't dated for the last two years, in fact have sworn off dating for ever, I didn't think you'd notice.'

But Kitty had noticed, was intensely aware of Sebastian Delfont. Even though there was a strict rule against establishing personal relationships with PWP clients. Even though it was true she'd sworn off dating.

She'd made that vow not just because of what had happened with the director, not because she'd lost her job and her reputation as a rising star in the PR world, but because her boyfriend had publicly doubted her word. To stand by her had meant he would be standing against his manager. He'd decided not to risk his own career in the company.

His betrayal had hurt her more than anything else—the doubts cast on her honesty, the slurs on her character, even the lurid headlines in the tabloids. All those fervent words of love, their plans for a future together, had been destroyed by the fever of her ex's ambition. How could she ever allow herself to trust in love again?

CHAPTER TWO

SEBASTIAN'S NEW HOME, the detached four-storey period mansion on Cheyne Walk, was magnificent. With a prime position on the Chelsea Embankment on the northern bank of the River Thames, it was worth untold millions. The building had come into Sebastian's family's hands as their townhouse more than one hundred and eighty years ago. But could he ever consider it home?

He stood in the new library, a former bedroom he'd had gutted to accommodate the custom-made bookshelves. Despite the changes, his grandfather's presence seemed to be embedded in the walls. The grandfather who had seemed to despise Sebastian's very being because his father had married against his wishes. Sebastian's beautiful, loving Spanish mother had been persona non grata and so, by extension, had been her son.

He had never felt welcome in this house. Both sets of grandparents had been against his parents' youthful marriage. His Spanish family had thawed somewhat when baby Sebastian was born. Not so his English grandparents.

His father had been on a gap year in Spain after he'd finished university when he'd met his mother, an art student who had been working as a barmaid. They'd married in a hurry when they'd discovered Sebastian was on the way. The day his parents had exchanged vows, his wealthy English grandfather had revoked his second son's trust fund. The birth of his grandson hadn't softened his stance.

Money had been very tight for the young couple, who'd existed on seasonal work that dropped dramatically at the end of each tourist season. In the hope of getting financial help, Sebastian's father had taken his baby son back to London, staying in this house. Even as a toddler Sebastian had sensed the hostility from his grandfather and a puzzling lack of affection from his grandmother. Weren't older ladies meant to swoop him up and smother him with kisses and cuddles?

By all accounts, the early years of his parents' marriage had been stressful, lack of money being a major issue, his father's homesickness and alienation from his family another. Several times, his father had taken him to London to try and forge a connection between his son and his grandparents, to seek help.

When he was nine years old his father had brought him here from their home in Barcelona to live for four months, the longest of any visit either before or after. The deal, brokered by his grandparents, had been that they would pay his father's tuition fees for him to study for a postgraduate teaching qualification, if Sebastian attended a private boys' school. His mother had stayed in Spain, working to help keep their little family afloat.

That had meant four months of seeing his mother only once at half-term break. Four months of his grandfather's harsh rules that had made him tiptoe around this house, terrified of angering the tyrannical old man. He simply hadn't been able to fit into the rigid mould his grandfather had tried to force him into—then or later.

In defiance of those expectations, he'd done very well treading his own path in the world of finance. He was independently wealthy. He'd never had to ask his grandfather for a penny. All the family obligations had fallen on the shoulders of his uncle, the first-born son, and his father, the 'spare' second son. The tragedy of both their premature deaths had established Sebastian as the reluctant heir. Although he had still been no closer to the grandfather who, it had seemed, would live for ever. Yet his grandfather had died six months ago—felled by a virus—and had left everything to Sebastian, his only living heir.

Sebastian's first thought had been that the inheritance was a hateful burden. He'd wanted to sell the house and put the memories it held behind him. And yet it was his heritage. Duty to his name, to his blood, reined in his impulse to shed them. He felt he owed it to his father and his uncle, whom he'd loved, to carry on the family traditions that had been so important to them both—despite the way his father had been treated. And he'd felt a link to the ancestors who had lived here since way back when his great-great-multiple times-great-grandfather had made his initial fortune in railways and textiles. Not all his ancestors had been the mean tyrant his grandfather was—he was proud to share their name.

'Knock-knock.' A sweet feminine voice interrupted his bitter memories of the past. Kitty Clements stood at the carved wooden doorway into the room. In her leggings and sturdy trainers, her cheeks flushed from exertion, she looked far from glamorous. But he couldn't remember when he'd last seen a lovelier woman.

'I wanted to check if you're happy with the way we stacked the bookshelves,' she said. 'Because if—'

The move to his late grandfather's house was proving to be not as traumatic as Sebastian had anticipated. He put that happy circumstance down to the cheerful, matter-of-fact presence of Kitty and Claudia from PWP over the last two days. Especially Kitty. Her golden hair and bright eyes seemed to bring sunshine to the darkest corners of the house and the sound of her laughter banished memories of angry shouted words. He realised his interactions with her were not about checking the accuracy of her work but about simply enjoying her presence.

'You've done a wonderful job,' he said. 'Perfect, in fact. Every book is in its correct place, exactly as planned. Thank you.'

She smiled. 'I'm glad. I knew how important it was to you to have everything just so.' Again, he had that feeling of an unstated but real understanding. She seemed kind. Not a quality he'd often found in the women he'd dated. 'It was a challenge, but satisfying. The work we did at the other end paid off.'

'I appreciate that,' he said. He also appreciated the way she behaved as if there was nothing unusual about his request. There would be a generous bonus going PWP's way.

Sebastian couldn't imagine that unpacking boxes and crates would be much fun, but Kitty gave every appearance of enjoying it. He'd like to ask her about her career before she'd become a person who packed but it would be inappropriate; she was what his grandfather would have called 'hired help'. He'd like to know her personal status too—she didn't wear a wedding or engagement ring but that didn't necessarily mean anything. She and her business partner, while pleasant and courteous, were careful to maintain a professional distance. But surely it must have been a job where she'd dealt with people, as Kitty was so warm and engaging. Retail? Hospitality? Health care?

'Thank you,' she said. 'We're on track to finish this afternoon. Let me know if there's anything else we can do for you before we leave.'

Kitty was leaving. Of course she was. He'd employed her to do a job and she'd fulfilled the terms of the contract most efficiently. He didn't know why he railed at the idea of saying goodbye to her, but he did. He tried to think of something that could delay her departure.

She glanced down at her watch. 'I would particularly like to leave on time today.'

Who did she go home to? A husband? Kids? A woman this appealing would surely not be single. Whoever held Kitty's heart would be a lucky man.

Sebastian felt saddened by the fact that, unless he decided to move house, he would never see Kitty Clements again. He didn't like that idea at all.

The light would go out when she left this house and he would be left to face the shadows on his own.

During her two years of business with PWP, Kitty had noticed the difference in people's attitudes towards the stages of a house move.

Packing up to leave was often tinged with sadness, especially if it was a move prompted by circumstances such as divorce or a landlord's whim. Even in the wake of a much-anticipated move there was angst about what to pack and what to discard. Countless times she'd had to unseal a taped box to accommodate an impulsive inclusion of something rescued from the give-to-charity pile.

Unpacking at the new dwelling, on the other hand, was sometimes a resigned acceptance of changed circumstances but more often a time of excitement at new beginnings. Of people rushing about oohing and aahing as they fitted belongings from an old life into an exciting new one.

Not so with Sebastian Delfont. His new home on Cheyne Walk was, hands down, the most amazing house she'd ever seen. And in her former life in public relations she'd seen inside more than a few grand residences, used for location shoots and product launches. Sebastian's house was four storeys of traditional luxury, high ceilings, ornate staircases and spacious rooms furnished with priceless antiques. It faced the Thames, glorying in a part of London that boasted the millionaire postcode of SW3.

Yet in the two days she'd spent there unpacking, her client had showed little excitement at his change of circumstances. His attitude seemed decidedly glum. Kitty couldn't understand why. Did he have no idea how the other half lived? How fortunate he was? Her entire rented flat where she'd lived in Camberwell would have fitted into one of the reception rooms.

Since the day she'd first met him she'd seethed with curiosity about this gorgeous man. Spoiled rich boy, so used to this level of privilege and wealth it simply didn't make an impression? Perhaps. That would go with the posh accent. Yet he struck her as being more down-to-earth. For one thing, he'd organised coffee and tea for her and Claudia in the vast old-fashioned kitchen, which was not something all clients thought to do.

She stood facing him in his refurbished library, the only newly decorated room in the house, having passed his inspection of the books placed in their correct order.

'What next?' she asked. 'I believe you have the people we recommended coming to hang your pictures tomorrow. We've stacked them against the walls in the same places they were hung in your Docklands apartment. We've also sent them the photos of how they looked there.'

'Well done. I'd put them up myself but hanging pictures is an art form in itself.'

'That's a good way of putting it.'

Kitty paused, knowing she shouldn't be chatting with him, but unable to stop herself. There was something about this man that interested her. Okay, be honest, attracted her. She couldn't deny that he'd occupied rather too much space in her thoughts than a client should. But she'd never see him again after today. She didn't move in the same elite circles as people who lived in Cheyne Walk.

She indicated the paintings in this room, lined up along the wall. 'I love those pictures. They bring a splash of Mediterranean colour into gloomy old London. Where are they from?'

'The island of Mallorca.'

'Gorgeous,' she said.

'I think so,' he said.

There was another question she ached to know the answer to and this was her last chance. 'I notice you have a lot of books here by Marisol Matthew. My grandmother loved romance novels and was a real fan of hers. I also loved them. With all those books on the shelf, you must be a fan too.'

'You could say that,' he said.

His tone was oddly neutral but still Kitty ploughed on; if she didn't, she would always wonder about the presence of those books on this man's shelves.

'When my gran was ill, she got me to read her favourite books out loud to her. Her very favourites were by Marisol Matthew; they were a great distraction in her...in her last days.'

She cursed under her breath. What had possessed her to say something so personal? Claudia would want to fire her. She wanted to fire herself. Personal details unwisely shared could be used as ammunition; she knew that only too well.

'She would have liked that.'

Kitty looked up at him. 'You knew her?'

'Marisol Matthew was my mother,' he said.

Kitty was so taken aback she struggled to find words. 'Your mother?' was all she was able to stammer out. 'I... I had no idea.'

'Why would you?' He politely didn't state the obvious: that she knew nothing about him either. 'Her true identity was a well-kept secret.'

Kitty knew the author had died some years ago; her grandmother had mourned the fact there would be no new books.

'Really and truly? Marisol Matthew was your mother?'

He smiled. Kitty realised it was the first time she'd seen him smile. It was the merest lifting of the corners of his mouth, but it lit his grey eyes and lightened his expression. He was even more handsome than the handsomest of the heroes in his mother's books. She caught her breath as awareness tingled through her.

'Really,' he said. 'I'm very proud of her. Of both of them. Not many people knew, but she worked with my father on her books. She came up with the stories and the characters and he helped her with the English as it wasn't her first language. Her name was Maria and his was Matthew. Marisol is a combination of Maria and the Spanish word for sun.'

'Was she Spanish? I only ask that as she wrote about such wonderful Spanish heroes.' But none so utterly gorgeous as her son. The thought intruded, despite Kitty's insistent jumping down on it.

'She was very Spanish.' His smile deepened.

'And your father was English?' She paused. 'Of course he must have been.'

He nodded. 'Matthew Delfont.'

She should leave it at that; she'd overstepped the boundaries already. But Kitty felt an urgent desire to grab as much knowledge about this intriguing man as she could while the clock ticked down to her departure.

'Did your parents live here?'

'No. But my father grew up in this house.'

'And you?'

He scowled. 'Only briefly.'

'Oh,' she said, realising that she might have strayed into a story where she had no right to be. But she couldn't help but register that he looked even more handsome in an intense, brooding way when his dark brows drew together in that forbidding scowl. She wondered whether he always wore black, because it certainly suited him.

'This was my grandfather's house. He died six months ago and I inherited.'

'I see,' she said, not at all certain she did or even wanted to.

'He and I did not see eye to eye,' he said. 'He was somewhat of a tyrant.'

A *tyrant*. Her own grandfather was kind and

thoughtful. She couldn't imagine having a tyrant for a grandfather and she itched to know more about Sebastian Delfont's fascinating family. But Claudia would be here any moment for their final wrap-up of this job. Enthralling as she found this discussion, she had to quickly change the subject. The conversation had definitely strayed way too far into the personal.

She took a deep breath and forced herself to sound practical and professional. 'This beautiful old house will need a lot of maintenance,' she said. 'Have you got all your household staff in place?' Imagine having a place where you needed household staff. It was a world she was getting an outsider's glimpse into.

'Not yet. There was a mass exodus after my grandfather died.'

'They were loyal to him? To someone his own grandson calls a tyrant?'

'Whatever his other faults, his staff were loyal. They wanted to retire. The live-in housekeeper was here for as long as I can remember. She was practically fossilised.'

A housekeeper. Kitty's imagination sketched images of a stern lady dressed all in black with the keys to the household kept on a chain around her waist, or someone round and jolly but with a firm hand, presiding over a 'downstairs' domain. She had no real-life experience of a housekeeper. Friends with busy careers had household help, but no one she knew had an actual live-in housekeeper.

'Your grandfather must have paid them fairly.' She knew only too well that loyalty could be bought.

'The salaries seemed above board, and they each retired with a good pension.'

In that case, if the staff were looked after properly, perhaps she could help. It wasn't the first time a client had moved into a new home and felt overwhelmed at the thought of getting it in shape. 'I can recommend Maids in Chelsea if you're looking for staff. They're an excellent agency. Quality people, credentials all checked.'

'Thank you,' he said. 'I'll note that.'

She glanced down at her watch. 'If there's nothing else, I'll finish up.' She paused, knowing there was no scope for a personal goodbye. 'Thank you for giving PWP the business. It's been a great assignment for us.' She wouldn't forget Sebastian Delfont in a hurry.

'You've exceeded all expectations,' he said.

She looked up at him, and for a long moment she met his steady grey gaze. Was there a hint of interest in her there, echoing her own interest in him? She felt overwhelmed by a pang of melancholy for something she could never explore, not with this man.

Flustered, she dropped her gaze, risked another personal comment, talking too fast, tripping over her words. 'I'm going to go home and reread my gran's Marisol Matthew books. She would have been thrilled to know I've met the author's son.'

'As my mother would have been thrilled to have such an avid fan. You have your grandmother's books at home?'

'I actually live with my grandfather and all her books are still there.' It was only a year since Gran had died and neither she nor Gramps could bear to change anything that would eradicate her presence.

'You're not married?'

Kitty choked on her surprise. 'Er…no.' And not likely to be any time soon. This was the first time she'd experienced even a twinge of attraction to a man since the disaster with Neil.

'Children?'

'I'll say no to that too.' She was twenty-eight; there was time for that yet. If she ever got the man right, if she ever trusted someone enough to commit. 'What about you? Are you married?' There had been no evidence of a wife or children in either of his residences, but you never knew.

'No,' he said. 'No ties.'

Again Sebastian held her gaze. A tremor of excitement rippled through her. Was he going to ask her out? She'd say no. Of course she would. It was impossible. He was a client. They came from different worlds. But he was *so* attractive. Surely rules were meant to be bent? Especially when she'd been the one to impose them.

'The reason I ask—' That voice! So deep and, well, yes, sexy.

Kitty felt herself swaying towards him in anticipation. She held her breath, was conscious of her heart beating so fast he could surely hear it. 'Yes?'

'—is I'm in dire need of an excellent housekeeper I can trust, and I think you'd be perfect. I'd like to offer you the job.'

CHAPTER THREE

SEBASTIAN THOUGHT HIS off-the-cuff idea to offer Kitty Clements the housekeeper's job had been an excellent one. Not only had he realised he needed help with this house, the idea had been a spur-of-the-moment brainwave to ensure he would see her again. However, as soon as the words left his mouth, he realised he might have made a very big mistake. In fact she might have taken his well-intentioned offer as an insult.

Kitty's blue eyes widened as she stared up at him for a long moment. 'Me? A housekeeper? Are you kidding?' Her tone was more abrupt than he might have expected. 'I'm not known for my housewifely skills.'

He frowned. 'But you're brilliant at packing.'

'Different skill set altogether.' She started to say something then stopped. 'You really don't want to know about the fuzzy things growing in my refrigerator. Or the fact I've been known to go out and buy underwear because I'm so behind on my laundry. Or—' She smiled but it seemed forced. 'I'll leave it there.'

Sebastian was glad she had. He didn't want to think about Kitty in her underwear. More to the point, if he let his thoughts stray that way he might think about Kitty without her underwear. Specifically, about him slowly peeling off said underwear, exploring the curves teasingly concealed by that long, baggy T-shirt.

'What exactly is the skill set required for a housekeeper?' he asked.

Kitty shrugged. 'I haven't a clue. I've never been fortunate enough to have one.'

'Neither have I,' he said.

'Really?' Her eyebrows rose in obvious disbelief. 'What about the housekeeper here who retired?'

'My grandfather's housekeeper. Employed by my late grandmother heaven knows how long ago. The only thing I needed to know about Mrs Danvers—that was my father's name for her—was how to stay out of her way. I visited this house on and off through my childhood, actually lived here for a while when I was nine years old. She didn't appreciate having an active little boy underfoot. I found her terrifying.' When he thought back to his time here, the house had been full of scary old people. No wonder he'd hated it.

'What about your parents?'

'Never. For one thing, they couldn't afford a

housekeeper. My parents married very young, against my grandfather's wishes. Her family weren't happy about the marriage either. They struggled in their early years.'

'I see,' Kitty said.

Of course she couldn't possibly understand. Like others, she would see the trappings of his wealth, both earned and inherited, and make assumptions. But he'd shared enough of his family history. 'For another, my mother would have seen employing one as an affront to her housekeeping skills. And she made certain my father and I pulled our weight with household chores.'

'Just like an ordinary family,' Kitty said. 'I mean a family who doesn't live in a house like this.' She indicated the grandeur around her with a sweep of her hand. 'You could hardly call this ordinary.'

'But not mine,' he said. 'At least not until recently.'

Her eyes narrowed. Suspicion looked cute on her. 'What about your fabulous apartment in Docklands?'

'Mine, yes.'

'I didn't see so much as a spot of dust when we were packing. Did you do the housework yourself?'

'A team of commercial cleaners once a week. Efficient and anonymous.'

'The kitchen was pristine. The plastic wrapping was still on the oven door.'

'Why bother to cook when I was surrounded by restaurants and food delivery services?'

'Same in Chelsea,' she said. 'Restaurants galore.'

'Yes,' he said. 'But my life will be different here. More obligations. I'll be expected to entertain, to live a more public life.' A life he had never sought, but had promised his grandmother, practically on her deathbed, that he would take up. 'And the house needs to be brought up to date.'

'I know what you mean about the house.' She looked around her. 'It's beautiful but a touch... not outmoded—that's not the right word—not gloomy, that's not the right word either.'

'An old person's house?'

'Not that either, although I know what you mean. But the rooms I've seen are so elegant and spacious, the antique furniture so timeless, maybe it simply needs to be lightened up.'

'What would you do with the house?'

'Me?' She looked startled. 'I'm no interior designer.'

'But you must see inside a lot of houses in your line of work.'

'To be honest, your house is one of the most beautiful I've been in. You wouldn't want to ruin its character by modernising it too much. Perhaps change the curtains from heavy dark velvet to linen or silk. Replace some of the wallpapers. Swap out the dark carpets for something fresher. That would make an immediate difference.'

'How would I go about that?'

He honestly didn't know. The Docklands apartment had been brand-new when he'd moved in. All he'd had to do was order the furnishings and make sure there was a place for his cherished possessions. He'd easily replicated that library here by giving measurements and photos to a decorator recommended by his father's lawyer, who'd been unimaginative but good at following orders.

He'd never allowed himself to get attached to places, or people for that matter. Too often as a child, as his parents followed seasonal work, he'd been torn away from rooms he'd settled into, a school where he'd made friends, a neighbour's dog he'd grown to love. As an adult he'd had more control over his life and this library, in some form, had gone with him—to his room at his uncle's house when he'd moved for university, to the rented apartments where he'd lived until he'd bought in Docklands. His obsession with keeping it just so had been a source of cruel amusement for Lavinia—which had only made him more obsessive about it, about his other possessions that had significance.

'Employ an excellent interior designer who would respect the history of the house,' Kitty said.

'You should get them to update the kitchen and bathrooms too.'

He nodded. 'You mean put my own stamp on the house?'

'Rid it of your tyrant grandfather.' Again that understanding from Kitty that he didn't expect.

'There is a lingering sense of his presence,' he conceded. The Spanish side of him felt something the pragmatic English side of him couldn't really acknowledge.

Kitty paused. 'I haven't got a psychic bone in my body and don't feel any kind of presence. Except that feeling of the lives who have gone before us you find in any old house.'

'That's reassuring,' he said, not sure whether to take her seriously or not.

'But, just in case, you could have a smoking ceremony. I believe you burn sage and wave it around to dispel lurking malevolent spirits.'

A grin tugged at the corners of his mouth. 'He was ghastly, but I don't know that I'd describe my grandfather as lurking and malevolent.'

'But you want to banish him just the same. While at the same time preserving the heritage of the house.'

'Exactly.'

'Think about the sage,' she said with a half-smile.

She glanced down at her watch and Sebastian felt a stab of panic. It was vital he did something to convince her to work with him. Of course he could just ask her out to dinner, but that would take interaction with her to a level he wasn't yet prepared for. His attraction to Kitty had come from nowhere. His mother had made a career out of instant attraction in her heroes and heroines. That was okay in books, not in real life.

Sebastian had grown more cynical when it came to relationships. In real life he had to be more considered. He'd learned his lesson with Lavinia. Uncle Olly had been quite the party animal and when Sebastian had moved to London for university he had always included his nephew when he'd been entertaining. The gorgeous brunette had been part of Uncle Olly's social set, two years older than Sebastian, seductive and sophisticated. He'd been instantly besotted—and he'd completely misjudged her motives. If he'd been more cautious he wouldn't have found himself trapped in an engagement he hadn't really wanted.

He didn't trust the sudden attraction to Kitty. He needed to test this feeling. Give it time. Get to know her. Be certain. And see if she felt it too.

'On second thoughts, I believe it isn't a housekeeper I need,' he said. 'It's more of a household manager.'

'Not someone to scrub the bathrooms and cook your meals? I warn you, I'm not great at housework.'

'No,' he said dismissively. 'A person who could

oversee what needs to be done, find the people to do it.'

'So hire the bathroom scrubber and the cook?'

'And the gardener too. Most importantly, the interior designer you suggest I need. And work with me to make sure it happens.'

She crinkled up her nose in a way he found delightful. 'And you seriously think that person could be me?'

'You've proved yourself to be formidably organised and efficient. And those ideas you've just outlined make sense.'

'But I know absolutely nothing about your needs.'

'My needs?' Needs of a kind that had nothing to do furniture or wallpaper and everything to do with this lovely woman came immediately to mind. The sudden flush high on her cheekbones made him aware her thoughts might have followed a similar path. *Interesting*.

'I… I mean your preferences, your likes and dislikes when it comes to furnishing and decorating and food too, I guess. But it's a moot point. I have my own business. I don't need to be your household manager, or anyone else's for that matter.'

Sebastian had a convincing argument right on the tip of his tongue. He really wanted Kitty to work with him. And not just because he found her so attractive. So why did Claudia have to breeze in at that moment? He smothered a curse word. There was an exchange of glances between the two women that he didn't understand. What did that little nod on Kitty's part mean?

Claudia looked from him to Kitty and back again. 'Did I just hear you offering my business partner a job?'

'No,' Kitty said.

'Yes,' he said. 'I need a household manager and I believe Kitty has just the right skill set for it. I'm prepared to pay more than the going rate, whatever that might be. What do you think?'

Kitty looked a touch bewildered at the speed his idea was progressing. He didn't mean to steamroller her. But the more he thought about it, the more he realised how much he needed her in that role, wanted her in that role. Because, although he'd only known her for a few days, instinctively he trusted her. And trust didn't come easily to him.

Kitty looked up at Sebastian as she considered her reply. Thank heaven she had somehow managed to conceal her utter embarrassment and searing disappointment at mistaking his intentions. There she'd been, entertaining a crazy idea that he was going to ask her out. Instead, he had placed her squarely in the 'downstairs' part of the 'upstairs/ downstairs' equation. Weren't people of his class notorious for doing that? Not that she liked to believe such a thing as class existed these days, but his accent and obvious extreme wealth seemed to place him in a different strata from her.

The role of a housekeeper—even when cleverly worded as 'household manager'—brought with it certain implications. The main one being a deeply ingrained imbalance of power—more so even than the office scenario of which she'd fallen foul. Her attacker had taken full advantage of the fact he'd been in a position of power over her. She couldn't get caught in that terrifying trap again. That was the joy of being her own boss. She and Claudia had agreed when they started working together that if one of them felt uncomfortable with a client—male or female—they would not work with them. An instant out was guaranteed.

Not that she felt uncomfortable with Sebastian. Far from it. Not only did she find him almost insanely attractive, but she liked him. Liked him more than she could have imagined liking someone on such a short and limited acquaintanceship. But she didn't want to be at his beck and call.

'I'm flattered. The job interests me. I would love to help give this house a facelift and help you, as you say, put your stamp on it. But I like being my own boss. I'm not looking to be employed ever again. And I wouldn't let Claudia down by leaving our company.'

'Let me try a different tack. I hired you to pack

for me on a contract. What if I were to offer you a contract to be my household manager?'

'You mean contract for Kitty's services through PWP?' said Claudia.

'Exactly. A short-term contract. Say six weeks, with an extension to be negotiable.'

He named a fee that made Kitty gasp. She had to disguise the gasp as a cough, so she didn't show her hand in a possible contract negotiation. Her hand being a need for extra money. Gramps was in a rehab hospital after having fallen and broken his leg. She was working with the health service to make his house safer and more old-person-friendly for when he got home. But she was paying to remodel his dated bathroom for safer shower access. That extra money would really help.

'I think we could spare you for six weeks,' Claudia said. 'We've got some good freelance packers in place to handle the rush of people wanting to move before Christmas.'

'That's true,' Kitty said.

She couldn't help but feel excited at the prospect of working for six weeks on something more creative than packing boxes. And she would still be able to stay under the radar. Who would expect the so-called notorious seducer and accuser of an innocent married man, Kathryn Clements, to be working as a household manager in one of the poshest parts of London?

Despite the hideous headlines and the hostility from her former employer, there were people who believed her about the assault. She firmly believed she would be vindicated one day. Living and working anonymously in central London would make it easier for her to keep in touch with those people and continue her discreet search for other victims of Edmund Blaine. He'd be exposed one day for the monster he was. She had to believe that.

She turned to Sebastian. 'If—and it's a big *if*—I took the job, would I be able to work after hours on admin for PWP with Claudia?'

'We're talking normal working hours,' he said. 'If you want to work on your business in your own time, I don't see a problem.'

'Do you intend this to be a live-in position for Kitty?' Claudia asked in her best client-interviewing tone.

'There is the housekeeper's apartment on the top floor or a downstairs guest room with her own bathroom at her disposal if she wants it,' he said.

Claudia turned to her. 'Great idea, Kitty. You told me there will be dust and disruption when you start renovations on your grandfather's house. Isn't the builder about to tear the bathroom out so you can get it all done by the time he's out of rehab?'

Six weeks living rent-free on Cheyne Walk, one of the most desirable addresses in London? She should jump at the chance. Six weeks working shoulder to shoulder with a man as attractive as Sebastian Delfont? Dangerous, perhaps. Not when she was attracted to him and he saw her as staff.

'Let me think about it overnight,' she said.

CHAPTER FOUR

NEXT MORNING, KITTY made her way through the security gate and up the hedge-bordered pathway to stand at the top of the marble steps outside the glossy black front door of Sebastian's house. Her breath clouded in the chill of the late October morning and she stamped her feet in their fine leather boots. She had spent a sleepless night thinking about Sebastian's offer and wanted to give him her decision today. She nodded to the courier standing by his bike, also waiting for the door to open. 'Can I take the parcel in for you?' she asked.

'Thanks, but no,' he said. 'Legal documents here. They have to be signed for by the recipient.' He looked at the address. 'Sir Sebastian Delfont.'

Kitty's mouth went dry. '*Sir* Sebastian?'

'Lot of sirs and ladies living around here. Dukes and duchesses too. You waiting to see him?'

'Uh, job interview,' she said, still reeling from the revelation of Sebastian's title.

'Good luck,' he said.

The door opened to frame Sebastian—*Sir* Sebastian. He was in black again, superbly cut trousers, a linen shirt that emphasised his broad shoulders, clean-shaven, even more handsome. Her heart thudded a warning: *danger.* She should not acknowledge her attraction to this man, even to herself. It could go nowhere.

He nodded at Kitty with a slow smile that sent a shiver of awareness through her. 'Glad you could make it.' He turned to the courier. 'I need to sign for that.' The courier handed him a large envelope and waited for Sebastian—*Sir* Sebastian—to sign. Kitty watched Sebastian give him a generous tip. The courier waved her a cheerful goodbye as he rode off.

She shivered. Perhaps from the cold, perhaps from trepidation.

'Come in; it's freezing out there,' he said.

Warm air enveloped her as she stepped into the marble tiled foyer. The beautiful old house seemed to be somehow welcoming; she had no feeling she wouldn't fit in there. In a downstairs role, she reminded herself, not as Sebastian's guest. No lingering malevolent spirits had haunted her while she'd been unpacking Sebastian's possessions. She still occasionally dreamed of her parents, taken from her by a drunk driver on the wrong side of the road when she'd been fourteen, but they were a loving presence and she woke from those realistic dreams feeling comforted and happy. It seemed

Sebastian's grandfather had been more the stuff of nightmares.

Sebastian went to help her as she shrugged out of her coat. Kitty gave into a little shudder of pleasure as his hands brushed her shoulders. Thankfully, he mistook it for a shiver of coldness.

'You'll warm up quickly; the central heating seems to operate as it should.'

'It's lovely and toasty, thank you, Sir Sebastian.'

He paused, her navy coat over his arm; her favourite red one had been banished to the back of her wardrobe—red drew too much attention.

'It seems strange to hear you call me that,' he said. 'I'm still getting used to it.'

'Really?' Kitty wondered why he hadn't mentioned his title in his dealings with her and Claudia. She had mixed feelings about it. It deepened the social chasm between them. At the same time, a reference for PWP from Sir Sebastian Delfont rather than Mr Delfont would hold greater sway in the competitive London market.

He hung her coat in the coat cupboard and turned back to face her.

'My grandfather was Sir Cyril. The title should have gone to my uncle, the first born, or my father, the younger brother. They both died too early to ever be Sir Oliver or Sir Matthew and their... their deaths brought the title to me.' He paused in an obvious effort to keep his voice on an even keel. 'It's my birthright, going back to my ancestor who made a fortune from the railways and had a baronetcy conferred on him for his loyal support of parliament.'

So Sebastian was a hereditary baronet. Her training in public relations had taught her how to address people from all walks of life, and the British honours system could be tricky to navigate. To her understanding, a baronet ranked below a baron but above a knighthood.

'That is a long history,' she said slowly. He'd been born into such privilege. Her history was peopled with hard-working everyday folk; her parents had met at university, each the first of their families to get a degree. 'I noticed the round blue plaque on the house honouring John Delfont, the nineteenth century artist who lived here. He was famous for his London landscapes, wasn't he?'

Sebastian nodded. 'There appear to be two streams of talent running through my father's side of the family. The majority of the Delfonts have displayed a remarkable skill for making money. But every generation also kicks up creatives like John Delfont, my great-great-aunt Betty, who was a star of musical theatre in the nineteen-fifties, actors, opera singers, writers, and my father, of course, with the Marisol Matthew duo.'

'And you?' Kitty asked. 'What stream of the family talent do you swim in?'

'Hands down the money-making. Thankfully, I excel at that.' His mouth twisted. 'I never want to be poor again, like I was as a kid, or dependent on the good graces of a tyrant like my grandfather.'

He waved his hand to encompass the ornately framed paintings on the walls of the foyer, the enormous crystal chandelier that made Kitty shudder at the thought of cleaning it. 'And now I step into all this, my heritage going back so many years.' He paused. 'But sometimes I feel like an imposter.'

'You don't look like an imposter.' The words slipped from her mouth before she could stop them.

'What do you mean?' he said.

'You look…born to the part,' she said. She was going to say he was handsome and very well dressed, every inch the aristocrat, but feared that might sound flirtatious and she couldn't be perceived to be flirting with him. What she thought of as being friendly had been construed as a sexually charged come-on, according to her attacker's lawyers.

'I was and I wasn't. There was an heir and a spare; I was third in line. If my uncle Oliver had had children I would have been pushed further down the line.'

'I'm sorry,' she said. 'That you lost your father and your uncle and…and your grandfather.' And Marisol Matthew had died too. 'So much… so much loss.' She didn't feel she could ask for details.

'I wasn't prepared for all this,' he said with a sweep of his hand. 'Uncle Olly was the one schooled in the duties and responsibilities that come with it. That's why I need help. It's why I need you, Kitty. Have you thought about my job offer?'

There was a vulnerability in Sebastian's eyes that tugged at her heart, frozen hard and impenetrable since the day the man she'd loved, and thought she'd spend her life with, had told her he actually believed her boss had assaulted her but couldn't stand by her and put his career at risk.

She wanted to help Sebastian, who seemed to have so much and yet had lost so much, but she had to be careful to keep her head, and above all to protect her vulnerable heart.

Kitty stood just footsteps into the room, as if she wasn't certain she wanted to be there. Sebastian found it difficult not to stare at her in admiration. In a wrap dress and high-heeled boots, business-like-Kitty looked so very different from person-who-packed-Kitty. Subtle make-up enhanced the blue of her eyes and the lushness of her mouth. Her hair was up in a tousled bun and for a crazy moment he ached to tug it away from its pins and let it tumble around her shoulders.

'I've thought a lot about your job offer,' she said very seriously.

'And?' He held his breath for her answer, not knowing quite why it was so important to him.

'It interests me. But, before we discuss it further, there's something you need to know about me.'

'Something terrible?' he joked, thinking it would be impossible to believe anything terrible about Kitty Clements.

She looked up at him, the blue of her eyes intensified by the blue dress she wore.

'Yes,' she said.

That wasn't the answer he'd expected, and Sebastian wasn't sure how to respond. If it was something truly terrible, he didn't want to hear what she'd done. And yet if he was to employ her, he had to know.

'You'd better talk about it,' he finally managed to get out.

'I need to,' she said firmly.

He showed her to the small living room that led off the foyer. It was a feminine room and he remembered it had been his grandmother's favourite place in the house when he'd lived there. He'd desperately missed his mother, but he'd only had rare crumbs of affection from his grandmother, Lady Enid—she was too much in thrall to her husband, who hadn't wanted 'the boy' mollycoddled. Nonetheless she'd sometimes slipped him a few pounds in an envelope when Sir Cyril wasn't around and had always sent him a card at birthdays and Christmas with some crisp notes in it. Once, when he was twenty years old and living with his uncle Oliver, Lady Enid had showed up at one of his parties. Sebastian had been stunned at the witty, vivacious woman his grandmother was when she was away from her husband's sphere. He had laughed with her, even danced with her, felt sad for her that she'd allowed herself to be so stifled.

Then he hadn't seen her one-on-one for years, until his uncle's funeral. She'd been devastated by the deaths of both her sons and later had reached out to Sebastian, just weeks before she'd been felled by a massive stroke.

Kitty sat down on the blue and yellow chintz-covered sofa and Sebastian took the opposite sofa, a coffee table between them. An empty crystal vase sat on the side table, and he remembered how his grandmother had always filled this room with flowers as his grandfather hadn't cared for them elsewhere in the house. Now the scent in the room was from Kitty's perfume, sweet and floral and alluring.

Kitty tugged her dress over her knees as she leaned forward towards him. The dress was high-necked and long-sleeved, as if to cover as much of Kitty as possible. But it did nothing to disguise her curves.

'Tell me about the terrible thing you did,' he

said stiffly. Had he been fooled by her open face and honest manner?

'It wasn't so much what I did, except be a naïve young woman, but about what was done to me.' She sighed. 'Have you looked me up online?'

'Only when I was researching packing companies. Your reviews were outstanding.'

'Then you wouldn't know that, before we started PWP, I worked for Blaine and Ball Communications.'

'The public relations company?'

She nodded. 'I wasn't Kitty then; no one called me that childhood name but my family. I went by my full name, Kathryn—with a K—and I much preferred it. More grown-up and professional.'

But not as cute, he thought.

'I started there as an intern after I graduated from university. At the end of the internship I was offered a job as a trainee account executive.'

'Well done,' he said.

'I was beyond thrilled. It was awesome to be part of a prestigious company. I worked with brand names with deep pockets for public relations as well as boutique start-ups where we had to be really creative with limited funds.'

'Sounds challenging.'

'Challenging, but I loved the work and met so many interesting people. I thought I'd found my lifetime career.' She paused, and he could see she was struggling to find the right words. 'After a few years slowly climbing the ranks, I was promoted into a role that brought me into the orbit of one of the directors, Edmund Blaine. Charismatic, a PR guru. I was flattered when he took an interest in me and became my mentor, which involved quite a lot of one-on-one time with him. I…' Her voice wobbled and she had to take a deep breath to steady it. 'I couldn't believe how lucky I was to have caught his attention.'

Sebastian's hands fisted tight. Now he had a strong suspicion of where this was leading. 'He was a predator?'

She nodded. 'I didn't realise that, but I started to feel nervous around him. His comments got personal, laden with sexual innuendo in a joking way that I didn't find funny. But I was still relatively junior and he held all the power.'

'Did you complain?'

Her hands were trembling and she gripped them so tightly together her knuckles showed white. 'To him? I felt too intimidated. I spoke to my direct manager as I thought she'd be understanding. But no. I can still remember Hilary's exact words. "That's just Edmund being Edmund. Be nice to him. Laugh it off. He can make or break your career".'

Sebastian cursed. 'Did you take her advice?'

'I tried to avoid him but it was almost impossible.' The colour had drained from her face. 'Then one evening I was working. Too late I realised he and I were the only ones on the floor. He called me into his office on some pretext, pulled me down to his lap and…and let me know what he wanted.' She shuddered and paused to take a deep breath. 'I was shocked frozen for a moment but then I protested and tried to get away. But he held me so tightly I couldn't free myself. He told me he knew I wanted it, when I was very definite I did not. Then he tried to…to sexually assault me.'

Sebastian uttered a vicious curse.

'I didn't give consent to anything, let alone what he was trying to do. There was no one around to hear me as I screamed and struggled. He clamped one hand over my mouth to shut me up and…and attacked me with the other hand. He was so much bigger and stronger than me, I couldn't stop him. But there was a second when he let go of me to… to fumble with his zip and I found the strength to kick him hard in the shin and free myself. As I ran, he called after me that no one would believe me.' Her voice faltered. 'He was right. They didn't.'

'I'm sorry,' Sebastian said, knowing how inadequate the words were. Her pain, her disbelief, her *horror* at what had happened was etched on her face, in the way she'd bowed her head and hunched her body. His instinct was to reach out and lay a comforting hand on her arm. But unwarranted contact with a man she didn't know well would be totally out of order. 'I believe you.'

She looked up at him. Her brow pleated together in a frown. 'You do?'

'Why would you make up something like that?'

'I wish other people thought like you do.' Her voice was underscored with bitterness and the light in her eyes had dimmed. 'Next day I reported the assault. Nobody at the company believed me. My version of events was totally discredited. It came down to a "she said, he said" scenario. What the older, powerful man said was believed. No proof, you see, except my word and my torn skirt that they said could have been caught on a nail.'

'Terrible is the right word for what happened to you,' Sebastian said. 'Why did you think you needed to tell me?'

'Because it got worse. The story was leaked to the media. I was labelled a troublemaker who had tried to seduce a happily married man then bad-mouthed him when he rejected me. I lost my job. My reputation. Doors slammed closed to me in every PR company in the country. If you search Kathryn Clements online you'll find the most horrible headlines. You…you might think twice about letting the person they portrayed into your house.'

'You seriously think I would let the gutter press influence my decision? If I'd seen those stories I would have asked you for your side of the story.'

She looked up, her eyes huge. 'You wouldn't judge me?'

Sebastian seethed with suppressed anger. He

couldn't let her sense that anger in case she felt it was directed towards her, instead of the man who'd taken advantage of his power over her, and the company that had let her down.

'I've made my judgement. You were treated atrociously.' He'd seen this happen at the investment company he'd worked for after he'd graduated from university. The new female graduates were seen as fair game by some of the senior managers. 'I would have sought revenge,' he said.

She laughed a mirthless laugh. 'I didn't have the resources for revenge. I was twenty-six years old and the man paid my salary. There was no proof; the police told me I had no case.' She paused. 'But I can't believe I was the first girl this guy attacked. Or the last. I'm watching and waiting for the opportunity to clear my name.'

He leaned towards her. 'If you decide to accept my job offer, you have my word you will be safe in this house. I will never step over the line of what is appropriate between employer and employee. And I'll make damn sure anyone else working here does the same.'

She unclenched her hands. Her tentative smile was enough to restore the light to her eyes. 'Thank you. In that case, I accept your offer.'

A wave of relief swept over him. He hadn't realised just how much he'd wanted her to say yes.

'Excellent,' he said. 'When can you start?'

CHAPTER FIVE

'I CAN CARRY my own bags, really I can.' On Monday Kitty was back in Cheyne Walk after a weekend at her grandfather's house in Kent, getting things ready for the builders. She glared up at Sebastian, determined to start this first morning in his employ the way she meant to continue. 'These small suitcases are nothing compared to the boxes I haul around for PWP.'

'It goes against the grain to see you carrying heavy bags,' Sebastian said, glaring back. 'My father would never let my mother carry anything heavy. No gentleman would, he used to say.'

Kitty's glare softened. 'And you were brought up to be a gentleman, I can see that,' she said. 'My grandfather is the same. It grates on him that he's in his eighties and I want to take the burden off him rather than the other way round.'

'So you'll let me carry your bags?' Sebastian said with that hint of a grin she found so appealing.

'No, I won't,' she replied with her own smile.

'Then I won't insist,' he said quietly, and she knew he had in mind the story she had shared with him the week before.

'Thank you,' she said. For a long moment their gazes met and, as before, she was uplifted by the compassion she saw in his eyes. She averted her eyes to hide the rush of emotion it triggered—if only Neil had showed even a fraction of this stranger's understanding—and reached down to pick up the two compact suitcases she'd packed for her six-week stay. 'As I understand, I only have to carry these to the elevator that will shoot us up to the apartment where I'll be staying.'

'Follow me,' he said.

The elevator was small, installed no doubt at some much later stage after the building's construction. Kitty found even with her suitcases between them she was still too close to Sebastian for comfort. Not that she didn't feel safe with him in such confined quarters, it wasn't that at all, but rather that she felt so intensely aware of him. Of how tall he was, although in heels she didn't feel so diminutive beside him, how broad his shoulders, how heady his spicy scent, how determined he appeared to be to keep a respectful distance from her.

It was impossible to pretend away her attraction to him. But denying it was made easier because she was under contract as his employee. That fact put a barrier between them so formidable it could be a high wire fence topped with broken shards of glass.

The elevator took them to the top floor of the house and the one-bedroom apartment the previous housekeeper had lived in for years.

'It's lovely,' Kitty said, looking around the surprisingly roomy living room. The Arts and Crafts willow leaves wallpaper, ivory curtains, white woodwork and simple furniture made it cosy but elegant. Her grandmother would have loved it. The window framed a view over the streets of Chelsea.

'Are you surprised? The apartment was redecorated not so long ago. I told you my grandfather, for all his faults, treated his staff well.'

Just not his grandson, Kitty thought.

'I wasn't exactly expecting bare boards, an iron bedstead and a view of a sooty chimney, but it's very nice indeed for staff quarters.'

'I'm glad you approve,' he said drily.

The bedroom was restful in a soft blue, the bathroom more than adequate. The kitchenette had everything she needed to make a simple meal.

'I'll be very comfortable here, thank you.' More than comfortable. She could never in a million years afford to live in prestigious Chelsea. She'd have weekends off for the next six weeks. Visiting her grandfather would take up some of her spare time but otherwise she'd have a once-in-a-lifetime opportunity to explore this exclusive part of London. 'Thank you,' she said again, before realising such profuse thanks was overkill. She was here to work.

'There's an office for you on the ground floor.' He looked at his watch. 'Why don't you come down in thirty minutes?'

'Why not now?' she said. 'I can unpack this evening. If I'm going to help you put your stamp on the house, we might as well jump straight into it.'

Sebastian—*Sir* Sebastian—seemed disconcerted by her enthusiasm. Kitty remembered his obsessive placement of the books in his library. Did he like to work to a rigid timetable? Would any kind of spontaneity be a problem? Was he going to be *difficult?*

After what seemed like an overly long pause, he spoke. 'I like your attitude.'

'I only have six weeks,' she said by way of explanation. 'Within that time frame I'll only be able to start projects, not see anything substantial through to completion.'

'So we should get started.' He headed towards the elevator.

Kitty went to follow, then stopped. 'Wait. I'll get my laptop. Never too soon to start taking notes.'

The room Sebastian had designated as Kitty's office had been his grandmother's study. There was none of the dark stuffiness of some of the other rooms. Kitty admired the classic desk and bookshelves, duck egg blue walls, framed botanical art, oriental rugs in pastel tones. She itched to park her behind in the upholstered desk chair and start working from such a delightful base.

'What a beautiful room; I wouldn't change a thing in here,' she said. 'What did your grandmother—?'

'Lady Enid.'

'What did Lady Enid do here?'

'I have no idea. Household management, I suppose. Then there was her charity work; I've only recently discovered how involved she was. Remember I told you how the money-making stream and the creative stream run through the family? Lady Enid swam in a money-spending stream—not in a particularly extravagant way but in a generous way. It appears her life was pretty much devoted to the charities she supported through the family foundation named after her. She was an heiress in her own right from her wealthy family.'

'That's admirable,' Kitty said. Donations which no doubt resulted in considerable tax deductions for her husband, a cynical part of her whispered.

'Since she died a year ago there hasn't been a Delfont actively involved with the foundation. Now I have to take over her mantle and work with the board of trustees. I made a promise.'

Kitty looked up at him. 'Sounds like a big job.'

'But a worthy one and I'm committed to it. I've inherited other roles too. My grandfather sat on a number of commercial company boards and I'll need to decide which ones interest me.'

Again, Kitty wondered why he didn't show more enthusiasm for his inheritance. But, curious as she was, it was none of her business.

'You have your work cut out for you,' she said brightly. 'Let's get started on the part where I can help you.'

'One more thing before we start,' he said.

'Yes?'

'I looked up the sage smoking ceremony. It's called smudging. I could be open to it.'

Kitty stared at him for a long moment before she spoke. 'Seriously?'

He nodded.

'To banish any lingering tyrannical presence?'

'Exactly,' he said.

She wasn't sure quite how serious he was.

Sebastian was deadly serious about the smoking ceremony. At his mother's funeral, her distraught mother, his *abuela,* had said there must be a curse on the Delfonts. Why had his parents died so young? his grandmother had wailed. Why had they only been able to have one child?

His father had died in a boating accident. He'd been fishing with friends off the rugged coastline near Port Soller, the closest port to their farmhouse in Mallorca, when the boat's engine had exploded. There were no survivors. His mother had been inconsolable. Sebastian, at twenty-seven, had been devastated. More so when his mother, still in her forties, had donned traditional black mourning and withdrawn from life. She'd died six months later of a heart attack. His *abuela* swore she had died of a broken heart from the loss of the man she had adored since she was eighteen.

What about me? Sebastian had silently screamed. Wasn't he enough to keep his mother alive? Irrationally, he'd seen her death as another abandonment. For the four months he'd lived in this hellish house, all he'd had of his *mamá* had been phone calls and postcards and that one half-term trip back to Spain. At nine years old, he couldn't understand why the feud with his grandfather had kept her from her son. *Hadn't he been lovable enough?*

When Uncle Oliver died eighteen months ago, buried by an avalanche while skiing in Switzerland, followed by Lady Enid's fatal stroke, then Sir Cyril had been felled by a virus—like dominos falling—Sebastian had started to believe in the possibility of a curse. And the source of any possible malevolence had been his grandfather.

'I'll organise the logistics of holding a smudging ceremony,' Kitty said, straight-faced, he was pleased to notice. 'In the meantime let's do something more practical about erasing your grandfather's presence from the house by redecorating.'

'I'll take you to the dining room first. Lady Enid held an annual dinner party at this time of year for the trustees of the foundation and their partners. I'd like to revive the tradition.'

The last time he'd seen his grandmother she had urged him to get involved with her foundation, which disbursed funds to charities involved with childhood illnesses. She'd been unwell, but not critically so, and had expressed concern that it would be in trouble without her at the helm. With his grandfather still alive that couldn't happen; Sir Cyril had barely spoken a civil word to him at Uncle Oliver's funeral, even though Sebastian had been his heir. Now, with both grandparents gone, it was his duty to take it over and be a steady hand on the tiller.

He already knew Kitty well enough to know that she showed her emotions on her face. Excitement danced across her features as she surveyed the grand room with the carved rosewood furniture, crystal chandeliers, ornate swagged velvet curtains and deep red walls. When the curtains were open the windows overlooked the formal city garden with its clipped hedges and central fountain.

'What an utterly splendid room for your dinner party,' she said.

'Splendid, yes, but I find it oppressive,' he said. Overbearing, like his grandfather. Sebastian shuddered at the memory of Sir Cyril sitting at the head of this table and picking at a nine-year-old's table manners in his haughty, bordering on cruel manner.

'The colours are too strong for today's tastes, aren't they?' she said. 'Change them and I suspect the room would be as impressive but have a very different feel.'

'You could be right,' he said.

'As I said earlier, I'm no interior designer. But I do know someone who I think would be perfect for your house. Evelyn Lim has worked with some of the best high-end design companies, both traditional and contemporary, and has just struck out on her own. Shall I make contact and see if she's interested and, more importantly, available?'

'Please do,' he said.

'Because I'm guessing you want to hold this dinner party sooner rather than later?'

'I want to hold it in two weeks' time so it will have to be in this room the way it is now.'

'Not necessarily,' Kitty said. 'If you have enough resources, and enough money to fund those resources, you might be surprised what you can achieve in terms of transformation.'

'How do you know all this?' he asked. She seemed so competent and knowledgeable.

She shrugged. 'Working in public relations, you meet all sorts of people. I first met Evelyn when I was working with a paint and wallpaper client.'

Under that heading of 'all sorts of people' was

also a predator who had effectively destroyed the career she'd loved. Sebastian renewed his determination to never cause Kitty more grief by stepping over the line between employer and employee. He would wait out the six weeks getting to know her and then make a decision about where to take it from there. One thing he'd already realised—Kitty wasn't looking for a short-term fling. *Neither was he.*

Kitty typed out a few notes on her laptop and turned back to him. 'Perhaps we should look at the kitchen next?'

One of the few people in this house who'd been kind to Sebastian when he was a child had been the cook. After his interminable days at the private boys' day school where his grandfather had enrolled him, he would sneak down here knowing the kind woman would always have a treat for him. Not the almond and anise *carquinyolis* his mother baked which he'd missed so much, but buttery shortbread or chocolate chip cookies which were nearly as good.

The large Victorian room hadn't changed: the black-and-white-chequered flagstone floor, the imposing fireplace, the big black range, the scrubbed wooden table where he'd sat, well-used cooking implements hanging from a rack. There were no bitter memories here.

Kitty critically examined everything in the room. 'The appliances are all relatively new; in fact everything is in excellent condition. Much better than I thought when I first glimpsed it last week.'

'I like this room just the way it is,' he said.

'Me too; it's wonderfully Victorian and cosy. I can just imagine the delicious meals that have been cooked here over the years your family has lived here.' She paused. 'Which brings me to ask about your thoughts on a cook. Do you want someone to live in? Or a daily cook? Or no cook at all and use caterers for the functions you say you'll be expected to host?'

'Let me think about that,' he said. 'There's more staff accommodation on this floor. But there will only be me living here. And you for the next six weeks.'

'You don't need to count me in for meals,' she said hastily. 'There's a perfectly adequate kitchenette in the apartment.'

'Of course,' he said. 'However, there might be occasions when you want to share a meal with me.' He would make sure of it.

'Er…that would be nice,' she said, flushing high on her cheekbones, dropping her gaze. 'In the meantime I'll talk to Maids in Chelsea about your cook situation. As well as the other staff you need, of course. If they can't help me, they'll know who can.'

Sebastian paused. He knew whichever way his words came out, they could be misinterpreted.

'We should continue your tour of the public rooms but, before you talk to the interior designer, I want to show you my bedroom. I mean the master bedroom. I mean a room that needs total refurbishment.'

Inwardly, he groaned. To even put the words *bedroom* and *Kitty* in the same thought led him somewhere he would not—*could* not—go.

CHAPTER SIX

KITTY FOUND HERSELF mesmerised by the sight of the carved wooden four-poster bed that dominated the overly elaborate Victorian splendour of the master bedroom. *Sebastian's bedroom.* He stood slightly behind her, yet her mind recklessly conjured up images of him in the bed, lying naked between heavy linen sheets that rumpled around his hips, his chest bare, that lazy grin she liked so much playing around his mouth, *beckoning her.* The fantasy was so strong she took a step towards the bed, intent on joining him, then recoiled as she realised what she had done.

What was happening here? Her libido had been firmly disconnected since Neil's betrayal, frozen in the 'off' position. No man had aroused the slightest interest. Now desire came rushing back through every erogenous zone she possessed. Sebastian had given her no cause for these crazy imaginings. He hadn't even touched her. There had been not a touch nor a kiss, no hint of mutual attraction to ignite the fuse.

Abruptly, she turned around—to put out of sight the bed that triggered such powerful yearnings for a man she couldn't have—and bumped straight into him. For a moment her hand was on his chest, her gasp of surprise not just from the unexpectedness of it but also from the intimate proximity to his strong body, his intoxicating scent.

'Sorry,' she said, her cheeks flaming hot as she stumbled back. 'Sorry.' She was shaking and had to take a deep breath to steady herself. Dear heaven, she hoped none of the desire for him her fantasy had aroused showed in her eyes.

'Sorry,' he said, also taking a step back.

Awkward. Excruciatingly awkward.

He was her boss—on a temporary contract to be sure—but it meant they would always be on an unequal footing. Then there was the inescapable fact they were from different worlds—the chasm between the mansion on Cheyne Walk and her grandfather's semi-detached two-up, two-down in the Kent village of Widefield was so deep she could never see it being crossed. Not to mention that Kathryn Clements still needed to fly under the radar. Having any kind of relationship—even a casual sexual fling—with a man who must surely be one of the most eligible bachelors in London could put her back in the unendurable glare of a hostile media spotlight.

A casual sexual fling? Where had that idea come from? *Get a grip, Kitty.*

She took another step back from him, tried to gather her thoughts, make her voice sound normal.

'I don't care as much for this room as some of the others.' She remembered the word Sebastian had used to describe the dining room. 'It's oppressive with these deep colours and dark furniture.'

'I agree. I think it would give me nightmares, which is why I haven't slept in here.'

Her flush became hotter. 'You haven't?' Her voice came out like a squeak. So much for her vivid imaginings. She cleared her throat. 'I... I thought it was your bedroom.'

'Not until it's completely remodelled. This room will be first cab off the rank for the smudging ceremony, along with my grandfather's study. It was Sir Cyril's bedroom.'

Kitty looked around her, at the dark ebony wood dressing table, the heavily textured wallpaper. 'It looks like it might have been your grandfather's *grandfather's* bedroom.'

'Like a museum,' he said, again with a hint of that grin she found so toe-curling. 'But it's such a great space and has a huge dressing room and a bathroom. And just look at that view over the Thames. It interconnects with what was my grandmother's room, which is beautifully done. I think she must have had it decorated when she did her study.'

'It's awesome when you think of the continuity, generation after generation of your family living here. But I guess there might be a feeling of all those shadowy figures with their eyes on you.'

'It sounds creepy when you say that, but I like to think most of my ancestors would be benevolent. My father and uncle grew up here and…and I loved them dearly. I know my father didn't care much for this room either.'

'We'll get it exactly how you want. I promise you. If I can get Evelyn Lim on board, she'll talk to you in detail about your taste in colours and styles to ensure that.'

Please don't let him want to turn this fabulous—if dated—room into a stark grey space like his apartment in Docklands. That look worked brilliantly there, but would not here.

He paused. 'Should I not be speaking to you about my likes and dislikes so you can brief possible contractors or staff?'

Her mind segued immediately to wondering about his other likes and dislikes that had nothing to do with paint colour or fabric patterns. She had to shake her head to clear her thoughts. Was she still in a sensual stupor from her hallucination about Sebastian lying on the bed where he hadn't ever slept?

'Er…yes, of course. Can we set some time aside for that?'

'This afternoon, three o'clock, my office,' he said.

His office was also his library, the one where

she'd so painstakingly shelved his books into the correct order. He'd said he could never use the room that had been his grandfather's study. The more snippets of information he revealed about his family, the more intrigued she became.

'Right. That's a date.' She paused. 'Not a date. I…er…didn't mean that. I meant that's an appointment. In my diary.'

'I know what you meant, Kitty,' he said, and she had a horrid feeling he was trying not to laugh.

'Back to work then,' she said. 'I mean, I'm not telling you to get back to work. It's me who has to get to work. You know, calls to make and all that.'

'I'll see you at three,' he said and this time he grinned.

When Claudia called Kitty at lunchtime to ask how her first day of the contract with Sir Sebastian was going she could only say, 'So far, so good.' She couldn't confess even to her best friend she'd been having erotic fantasies starring Sir Sebastian starkers and how very disconcerting she found it.

Her awoken libido was nothing to do with her attraction to Sebastian, she firmly told herself. It was more likely her body was screaming at her that two years had been too long without a man. To be in close contact with someone as good-looking as her temporary boss had obviously awoken desires that had been too deeply buried for too long. If she had told Claudia, Kitty knew what her friend would have said: she needed to get dating again; by cutting herself off from men she was letting Neil win, letting despicable Edmund Blaine win.

When the six-week contract was over, she'd dip a cautious toe into the dating pool by signing up to some online dating apps. She'd never used one before, had never needed to. Her first boyfriend, Owen, she'd met in high school. That had ended when she'd set off to university in Nottingham. Dating disasters of the common student kind had followed. Until she'd fancied herself in love with an exchange student from Australia. The relationship lasted all the way through second year, at the end of which he'd gone home to Sydney. They'd vowed to make it work, but absence hadn't let their hearts grow fonder and her long-distance romance had dwindled away to nothing. She only wished him well and vice versa.

She'd met Neil on her first day of her internship with Blaine and Ball. There had been just the two of them in the intake and they were often in each other's company. He'd been fiercely competitive but a lot of fun, with the handsome, sporty kind of blond good looks she'd always found appealing. In retrospect, she sometimes wondered if he'd pursued her so relentlessly because other guys at work had shown interest and Neil couldn't bear to be perceived as a loser.

She'd let herself be picked up by his whirlwind of networking and partying and, before she knew it, they were exclusive. When her flatmate moved out, it had seemed the right thing for him to move in. Not just by default. He'd seemed as in love with her as she'd been with him. They used to have long discussions about what their future children might look like; baby names had been debated. It was understood that living together would lead to an engagement. She had never doubted him, even though he could be an outrageous flirt when he'd thought it might get him somewhere. He swore he'd never cheated on her and she'd believed him. But his ambition had come between them and when that whirlwind had changed direction she'd crashed out of it to land on her own, heartbroken, bruised and betrayed.

Yes, it might be time to release herself from her dating sabbatical and look at those apps. Although the insidious thought crept into her mind that there wouldn't be any men like Sir Sebastian Delfont around and it was he who had brought her libido to such a roaring awakening. What other man could possibly come close to him?

At three o'clock she sat opposite him at his desk in the room surrounded by his strictly ordered books and the beautiful paintings of a Mallorcan farmhouse and a citrus grove. She was glad of the distance the desk put between her and him.

Glad that it emphasised her position as employee. It was safer that way. Not safe from him, rather safe from her newly activated hormones.

'I've got some positive news to report,' she said, forcing herself to sound totally businesslike. 'First, Evelyn Lim is both interested and available. We're lucky. She was about to start on a major design job but the couple decided to divorce and sell the house, so Evelyn is unexpectedly free. If you want to move quickly on the dining room for your dinner party, she can meet with you tomorrow morning. Does that suit?'

'Perfectly,' he said. 'Only I want you in on that meeting.'

She nodded. 'Regarding your cook situation, I've thought somewhat outside the box.'

'Fire away.'

'I've found two well-trained chefs with impeccable references who are friends. Both have young children and would like to job share. I set up a conference call with them both. I liked them and think the job share could work.'

'How does working evenings tally with the cooks having kids?'

'It's up to them to sort out their childcare. In my experience, people who job share are keen to make it work. These two women know the role here entails lunch and dinner—if you remember, you said you'd get your own breakfast. And sometimes entertaining might call for working later into the evening. When would you like to meet them?'

'No need for me to interview the potential cooks. I'll leave it to you.'

Again, there was that indifference she was coming to expect from him. Again, she felt like shaking him. If she had the opportunity to have a cook prepare all her meals she'd be dancing on air.

'I appreciate your confidence in me.' She smiled her thanks. 'But when it comes to food, I really think you should be involved. Why don't we ask each of them to cook lunch here and see how you like what they come up with? Alisa can do tomorrow, Josie the day after. Does that suit?'

'I'll leave it in your capable hands.'

Capable hands. He'd meant it as a compliment but how boring it made her sound. Was that how he saw her? How very different from her fantasies about him.

'Finding a housekeeper might take longer, but I've got Maids in Chelsea and another very reputable domestic staff agency on the hunt for us. Once we've got a housekeeper, they can work with us on the other household staff.'

'As long as they're of the same calibre as my household manager. You've achieved so much in one day.'

'Thank you,' she said, unable to help from basking in the warmth of his praise.

'Thank *you*,' he said. 'You've exceeded all expectations already.'

'I'm pleased to hear that,' she said, not sure what else she could say. She felt suddenly shy with him and covered it up with a businesslike briskness. 'Moving outside the house to the garden. I've got some names from an agency specialising in gardeners and horticulturists, but I haven't interviewed them yet. To be honest, I know very little about gardening.'

'It's not my forte either.'

She sighed. 'I wish I could have my grandfather help me interview the potential gardeners and put them through their paces.'

'Your grandfather is a gardener?'

'He loves his garden and spends even more time in it since my grandmother died. He also has an allotment where he grows fruit and vegetables.'

Kitty wondered if someone as posh as Sebastian would know what an allotment was—a small plot of land leased from the council for a nominal fee for the express purpose of growing plants.

'Why not get your grandfather up to London to help you?'

'It's not as easy as that. Gramps refuses to admit he's in his eighties and has to slow down. He insisted no one but him could prune his favourite climbing rose, fell off the ladder he shouldn't have been up, fractured his leg in several places and is now in a rehab hospital.'

'I'm sorry; that sounds very painful.'

'As he puts it, his pride got a worse battering. He's working his way towards being able to go back home and live independently.'

'I hope all goes well for him,' Sebastian said politely. He paused. 'I would suggest getting help from the man who kept this garden in order for many years, as well as the country estate in Dorset. But he retired after my grandmother died and moved up north.'

There was an estate in Dorset? Of course there was.

'Was his name Albert?' Kitty asked. 'If so, he left a handwritten workbook, where he recorded the seasonal work done in the garden. It even has sketches. I found it in Lady Enid's office, surprising really as I thought it should belong in the potting shed. I'll refer to that when I interview gardeners.'

'My grandmother thought highly of Albert and left him a substantial legacy in her will,' Sebastian said.

'Really?' Kitty's imagination raced. 'You think they were friends?' More than friends?

Sebastian frowned, a stormy look that put Kitty back in her place. 'Delfonts don't make friends with staff. My grandfather would never have sanctioned that.'

Okay, make that *firmly* put back in her place.

'I understand,' she said, tight-lipped. *Only too well.*

Immediately, Sebastian realised he'd got it wrong—again—with Kitty. She was obviously offended by his pronouncements about Delfonts and their staff. Already he could read so clearly the emotions that skittered across her face.

'I was, of course, referring to my grandfather's generation of Delfonts. Not mine.' He pushed his fingers through his hair in frustration. 'It's taking me some time to get used to the fact I am now the sole Delfont—and my grandfather is certainly not my role model.'

In deciding to shoulder all his inheritance entailed, Sebastian had vowed he would be a different kind of baronet from his grandfather—one with morals and compassion, a baronet who would make his uncle Olly and his father proud, someone who could make a difference through his grandmother's foundation and the ethical way he did business.

'I understand,' she said, her mouth still turned down.

But could she? He would have to share an awful lot about his past and his toxic family interactions before she could begin to understand. And he wasn't prepared to do that. Not when it would reveal so much about himself.

No woman will ever want to live with you, his former fiancée, Lavinia, had shouted at him, after he had broken off their engagement.

According to the woman who had hidden her despicable hidden agenda, he was obsessive, too focused on work and stingy in that he'd refused to finance her excessive, extravagant spending sprees in the designer boutiques of Bond Street.

'You certainly know the value of a penny,' she'd sneered at him.

Actually, he did. He'd grown up in a family where, as a child, every *peseta* had counted, where he'd known what it was not to have the essentials. To crown her litany of complaints, Lavinia had accused him of being unlovable and unable to love. Ironic, as she'd been happy enough to pretend to love him, when really she'd been in love with the idea of one day becoming a Lady, with the Delfont fortune at her disposal.

But was he being fair to Kitty? She hadn't blinked at his compulsive need to have his bookshelves in order, in fact had reacted with rare understanding. She might understand how that boy who'd lived in poky rooms as the son of the seasonal caretakers in a block of Spanish holiday flats felt such a fraud as Sir Sebastian. There was no doubt that she brought light into the shadowy corners of his house. Could she do the same with his life? Dare he even let himself hope for such a thing? *Was he worthy of her?*

He leaned across the desk towards her. 'I actually don't think of you as "staff". You're an independent contractor helping me out. If we end up friends after all this, I'll be happy.'

One thing was sure, when she'd tripped in the master bedroom and bumped into him, friendship hadn't been his initial thought. She'd felt so good—her warmth, her curves—it had taken all his determination not to be that man who took advantage. For the moment she'd taken to steady herself, all he'd been aware of was how lovely she was and how much he wanted to pull her into his arms.

'Er…me too,' she said, although she didn't sound convinced.

Unwittingly, she'd hit a sensitive spot. His grandmother had summoned him after Uncle Olly's funeral to the Dorset estate where she'd been living. She'd been full of regrets that her grandson was virtually a stranger to her. It had been the start of a tentative reconciliation, when she had discussed her concerns about the Lady Enid foundation. The time had been poignantly precious as he hadn't seen his grandmother again.

Kitty had picked up on something he had suspected when he'd seen Lady Enid and her head gardener Albert together. There had been something there, definitely friendship, perhaps something more. His grandmother had told him she and Sir Cyril had led independent lives for a long time—or as independent as life could be married to such a domineering man. It had become obvious to him that his grandfather had been emotionally ill-equipped to manage close relationships of any kind—his wife, his sons, certainly his grandson. His grandmother had hinted that Sir Cyril's own father had been cruel, borderline abusive.

Had Lavinia been right? Had he inherited some kind of emotional inability to love? Because the disaster with Lavinia had made him realise he had never been in love. Not the kind of 'in love' that led to commitment and happy ever after. Was it even possible for him?

'As for your question about my grandmother, yes, I think she saw Albert as a good friend. Her marriage to my grandfather wasn't a happy one. Good for her if she found comfort with a man those in her social circle would deem totally unacceptable.' Like his family had found his mother unacceptable. 'Perhaps it was more than friendship; I don't know. I might be the son of Marisol Matthew but I'm not good at picking up on romance.'

Kitty's eyes widened. 'Perhaps it was a real-life romance. The more I hear about your family, the more fascinated I become. Maybe you could write a novel about them.'

'Huh,' he snorted. 'No one would believe it.'

He had written a novel. Two, in fact. Not about the possibly cursed lives of his wealthy family, but dark thrillers with a tortured detective hero. The manuscripts were sitting in a drawer. He'd written them in the sad time after both his parents had died and he was living with Uncle Oliver. There was no time for writing stories now, with his new duties to fill the days.

His phone buzzed with a message. 'Excuse me. I need to read this.'

'Of course,' she said.

Sebastian read the message with some relief. He looked over to Kitty. 'The executive assistant I approached has agreed to come on board. Guy Perrint worked with my uncle Oliver and is just the person I need.'

'That's good; I wondered if you would need an assistant.'

'And you're glad you didn't have to recruit him too?'

Her smile lit up her beautiful blue eyes. 'I didn't say that, but yes. I'm glad I can concentrate on getting your household in order.'

'That said, I need to spend some time on a call with him.'

'Now?'

'Yes.'

'But Evelyn Lim is coming in the morning and we'd scheduled to discuss the changes you want done to the house.'

'Can we do it over dinner instead?' He voiced the invitation without thinking about it, forgetting she might be averse to having anything to do with an employer outside of work hours.

It was the first time he'd seen her flustered. 'I… er… I'm not sure…'

'Not a good idea? I thought, as it's your first night living in the house, you might welcome a meal out. But of course I shouldn't be demanding overtime so quickly.'

'Overtime? I wouldn't see it as overtime.'

'There are some excellent restaurants within walking distance.'

She bit down on her lower lip. 'That's the thing. I can't risk being seen in a restaurant with you.' She flushed high on her cheekbones. 'I need to keep a low profile. It seems you're considered one of the most eligible bachelors not only in London but the whole of Great Britain. If you're noticed, so might I be.'

'I hadn't thought of myself like that,' he said, frowning.

'Handsome, wealthy, a title. I'm afraid you won't be able to escape media interest.'

'Which I most certainly don't want.'

'But you will need to court it if you want to move forward with Lady Enid's foundation. I'm speaking with my PR hat on here.'

'But not scandalous speculation about my private life.'

'Or mine,' she said.

Her eyes were downcast and her full lower lip

trembled. With good reason. Since their last conversation about what had happened at Blaine and Ball, he'd looked up some of the truly hideous stories about Kathryn Clements that had been splashed across the tabloids.

'I don't want to risk subjecting you to that again,' he said.

'Thank you,' she said in a very small voice.

'Perhaps a meal from one of those good restaurants delivered here and eaten in privacy might be a better idea?'

She paused and he thought she might refuse that idea too. But she nodded. 'A much better thought.'

'And now it's my turn to quiz you about your likes and…uh…dislikes.'

A sudden flash of what it might be like to explore her likes and dislikes in bed caused his voice to hitch. She was wearing a smart navy trouser suit cut in a masculine style, but it only served to emphasise her femininity and sensuality. Images of him slowly peeling off that suit, the shirt, the underwear beneath it to reveal pale skin flushed with arousal and blonde hair tumbling around her breasts tormented him.

Startled, she looked up at him. 'Me? Why?'

He banished the images, cleared his throat. 'About food,' he said hastily. 'Italian? French? Indian? Vegetarian? Vegan? For dinner, I mean.'

'Let me think,' she said.

Was there something in her eyes to indicate

she'd known exactly what he'd been thinking? And that perhaps the very same thoughts had crossed her mind regarding him?

He could only guess. That line between employee and employer he'd promised never to cross lay stark and strong between them.

CHAPTER SEVEN

KITTY WAS GLAD that Sebastian had suggested eating dinner in the basement kitchen rather than the elegant breakfast room, where the family had traditionally eaten casual meals, or in that grand, imposing dining room. The kitchen was altogether a more pleasant and welcoming space. Or was that because she felt more comfortable 'downstairs' rather than with the grandeur of 'upstairs'?

The kitchen was grand in its own way, with its size and the venerable age it wore with such dignity. She sat opposite him across the scrubbed oak table. She and Sebastian had laid the table together, searching through drawers for the blue and white checked tablecloth and the heavy china plates and serviceable cutlery intended for staff use over the years. Such an everyday activity had gone some way to break the ice between them—after all, she'd only known him for a week.

Even so, she had to pinch herself—here she was sharing a meal delivered from a fashionable restaurant in Chelsea with Sir Sebastian Delfont.

Surreptitiously, she darted a glance up at his lean, handsome face, shadowed with the sexiest trace of evening stubble, and her heart seemed to skip a beat. He had a sensuous mouth, full lips but not too full, the top lip narrower than the bottom—wonderful to kiss, she would imagine. He'd said he wasn't married. Did he have a girlfriend—lucky woman—or a string of girlfriends? She mentally shook herself out of that thought. She had to fight to keep her guard up, to remember this wasn't a date. *And to keep her erotic fantasies about this man at bay.*

It had been a unanimous decision to order Italian, although Indian had come a close second. Sebastian had said he would never eat Spanish food from a restaurant, as it could never compare with his *abuela's*—his grandmother's—cooking. Kitty had understood exactly where he was coming from. No one cooked roast beef and Yorkshire pudding the way her gran had, she'd told him. One thing, at least, they had in common, although it was a tenuous connection. She would struggle to find points of connection with Sebastian, their worlds were so very different, even beyond the upstairs/downstairs thing.

They enjoyed a minor battle of wills as Sebastian insisted Kitty have the last of the delicious antipasto selection they had ordered, while she thought he should have it. But she didn't need much persuasion to lay claim to the remaining bite-sized crostini topped with artfully placed Parma ham, Stracciatella cheese, rocket and pine nuts.

'This looks deceptively easy to put together, for something so delicious,' she said, eyeing it critically.

'Are you planning to replicate it?'

'Maybe. I might organise a little party for Gramps when he gets home from hospital. He's quite adventurous with food considering his age. Not that I'm anything but an everyday kind of cook.'

Everything she'd learned about cooking she'd learned from her gran. When she'd arrived to live with her and Gramps, the family were in deep shock and grief, Kitty from the loss of her parents, her grandparents at the loss of their daughter. Her uncle, their son, had come from Canada for the funerals but he had his own life there and had soon returned home. She hadn't been particularly close to her father's family in Norfolk; there'd been no question of her going to live with them.

Kitty had had to adjust to a very different life. Her beloved grandparents had become her parents too. Gran had nurtured her with home cooking, supplemented by the bounty from Gramps's allotment. Her grandmother had cemented their new bond by keeping her granddaughter close in the kitchen.

'Why do you live with your grandfather?' Sebastian asked.

Surprised, Kitty paused with the crostini halfway to her mouth. She put it back down on her plate. 'Why do you ask?' she said.

'It's common among my family in Spain for the different generations to live close by, but not so much here. You're a very attractive woman and I'm surprised you—'

'Don't live with a man?' she said.

'Yes,' he said.

'I've lived with a man and have no intention of repeating the experience any time soon.' She could hear the bitterness in her voice that rose like a poison whenever she thought about Neil in any context. Sebastian nodded in acknowledgment of what she'd said. He seemed unsettled by her change of demeanour, perhaps unsure about what to say in reply.

'I see,' he finally said.

She took a sip from her glass of mineral water in an effort to regain her composure.

A very attractive woman, he'd said. Were they just throwaway words, or did he really mean them? She certainly thought he was an attractive man. Exceedingly so.

She forced a more neutral tone to her voice. 'My grandparents brought me up after my parents died when I was fourteen.'

'I'm sorry,' he said, as people always did when

she told them about her childhood tragedy. She used the phrase herself, though sometimes wondered why she was saying sorry for something that had been quite out of her control.

She took another sip of her water. 'After the scandal erupted, I was left without a job and unable to pay the rent on my flat.' Neil had moved out, leaving her with the entire rent burden and the gutter press on her doorstep. 'I went home. And found not only did I need my grandparents, but they needed me. That's why I live with my grandfather.'

She picked up the crostini again. 'And I think Gramps would very much enjoy something like this.' There had been more than enough talk about her personal life and she hoped Sebastian would pick up on the change of subject.

'I'm sure he would enjoy it,' he said. 'I certainly did.'

'Why is Italian antipasto so extraordinarily good? I could eat an entire meal just from the antipasto table.'

He smiled. 'But then you'd be cheating yourself of the main meal, wouldn't you?'

When he smiled like that, it was impossible not to smile back—her smile tinged with relief that he hadn't further questioned her about her private life. The ending of her relationship with Neil had left her broken and with that had come an immense sense of failure—she'd meant so little to him that he'd chosen his job over her. If he'd ever loved her, how could he interact with her abuser every day?

'Our next course looks good too,' Sebastian said as he eyed the *ragu alla Bolognese* made with handmade tagliatelle. Kitty could see just by looking at it that the dish bore no resemblance to the humble spaghetti Bolognese she made and the smell of it was making her mouth water.

'We haven't done a lot of talking about your preferences for the meeting with the interior designer,' she said, daring to tease him a little without stepping over the formidable boundaries between them.

'Perhaps not for the interior designer, but certainly for the two cooks,' he said, looking longingly at the *ragu*.

'True,' she said with a smile. 'I've certainly garnered some clues about what you like in food. Italian, Indian, Greek, Thai, Spanish—but only when it's homemade—French, Chinese—'

'In short, any good food that I don't have to cook myself.'

'And plenty of it, I notice,' she added.

He was lean but strong and firmly muscled. She hadn't failed to notice that when she'd stumbled against him that morning. He either exercised a lot or was one of those people who ran hot and burned up energy. She had to tear her mind away from imagining how he'd look in nothing but sleek tight-fitting athletic gear.

'Exactly,' he said. 'What about you?'

'Does it matter what I like?' she asked, surprised.

'I hope this won't be the only dinner I share with you.' Kitty tried to hide her surprise, successfully she thought, as Sebastian continued without hesitation, 'And when our two cooks are on board—if we approve of them—I will expect them to make lunch each day, not just for me but for anyone working in the house, including you and my new assistant, Guy.'

So it wasn't personal, the sharing dinner thing. Just a benefit for the staff. She had no cause to feel disappointed.

'That's kind, but I don't expect—'

'You won't have to eat the meal if you don't want to, but it will be there if you do.'

He was generous and thoughtful and, not for the first time, Kitty wondered why Sir Sebastian wasn't married. There must be eligible women lined up along Cheyne Walk all the way to Battersea Bridge. But she wouldn't have this job or be here eating in his kitchen if he was married, she reminded herself. A wife wouldn't have hired the notorious Kathryn Clements to work with her husband.

'Okay, let's start on that *ragu* and the tomato and basil salad,' she said. 'But we really need to be prepared for the meeting with Evelyn Lim, especially if you want the dining room transformed in time for your foundation board dinner.'

'I need no second invitation,' he said. He started to serve her a generous helping of the wide-cut tagliatelle, coated with a rich, slow-cooked sauce.

She put up her hand. 'Whoa, that's more than enough for me.'

'Are you sure?'

'Absolutely,' she said.

It was an automatic response. Once she'd left home and her grandmother's home cooking to go to university, she'd enjoyed the freedom to eat what she wanted. That had meant too many convenience and fast foods, not to mention nights out at the pub with her friends. And she'd been more inclined to join drama and music societies than sports clubs. She'd stacked on the weight and it had been very hard to shift. That *Pretty, Plump and Predatory* headline had really stung, and not just for the predatory part. After the incident with Edmund Blaine she'd thrown herself into intense self-defence training. That, coupled with the appetite-destroying misery she had sunk into after her public humiliation, had seen her back at a more comfortable weight. But she was still vigilant with what she ate.

'All the more for me then,' he said with mock greed, which made her laugh as it was something Gramps would say. Who would have thought Sebastian, who had seemed so forbidding at first, would make her laugh?

The *ragu* was every bit as delicious as it looked and they only exchanged exclamations of appreciation as they ate. She put down her cutlery at the same moment Sebastian did and they both smiled. He was handsome whichever way she looked at him, but when he smiled his grey eyes warmed his serious expression and made him appear not just extraordinarily good-looking but also more approachable.

'You seem more relaxed down here in the kitchen,' she ventured.

His dark eyebrows rose, and for a moment she regretted her temerity in taking the conversation to something perhaps more personal than was warranted. The slow tick of the big farm-style clock above them on the wall dominated the sudden silence.

'Perhaps because it was the only room in this house I ever felt happy in,' he said finally. 'That was thanks to the cook. Fran. Her name was Fran. She was kind to a homesick young boy.'

'And other people in the house weren't?' Kitty said tentatively. 'Like…like the tyrant grandfather?'

'And the grandmother who didn't dare go against his wishes,' he said, his voice sombre, seemingly lost in memories that were less than pleasant.

Kitty held her breath. She was so curious about his story, but she didn't want to seem to be prying. Of course she'd looked him up on the internet but he wasn't on social media and there was virtually nothing, apart from a story about the death of his uncle in a skiing accident.

Finally, she decided to ask the questions. He didn't have to reply. 'You mentioned you lived in this house only briefly. Was that when you were nine years old?'

He nodded. 'For four months while my father was studying in London for his postgraduate teaching qualification. I had to go to school here. My mother stayed behind in Barcelona with her parents.'

'Your mother stayed behind? That must have been tough for you.'

His eyes darkened with, she thought, remembered pain. 'It was. For my parents too. But it wasn't the first time. Circumstances meant we were quite often separated as a family when I was a child.'

Kitty didn't say anything, hoping he would elaborate. She had a feeling he didn't talk much about his past; an ill-timed comment from her might pull him out of his memories.

'It wasn't just the need for them to go where the work was,' he said. He took a sip from his glass of wine, put it slowly down as if he were deliberating whether or not to answer her. 'My mother's health was uncertain. She had several miscarriages but no more babies. At times she had to have bed rest, and I was shunted around various Spanish relatives while my father had to work away. At the time, all I was really aware of was that I never got my promised baby brother or sister.'

Kitty's heart went out to him. 'I… I have some idea of how that must have felt. I'm an only child too. I longed for a brother or sister, but I was told it wasn't "meant to be".' She'd sometimes thought dealing with the death of her parents might have been less traumatic if she'd had a sibling.

'My *mamá* used to say I got all her love.'

Kitty smiled. 'I think I remember my mum saying the same thing.' She dared another question. 'Was your mother's health the reason she couldn't come to live here too with you and your father for that four months?'

'Not that time. My father needed to gain qualifications to get better paid jobs. My mother needed to work to help support our little family; she had a job in an art gallery she didn't want to lose. Besides, she wasn't welcome here, had never been welcomed here. That's why we lived in Spain.'

'Why was that?'

'My father married against my grandfather's wishes. My father was on a gap year in Spain after he finished uni. My mother was an art student working as a barmaid in Barcelona. They were very young. She always said she could write truthfully about love at first sight in her books because that was how it was for them.'

'How lovely,' Kitty said. The fan girl in her appreciated this was Marisol Matthew's own love story. It seemed surreal she should be hearing it from her son.

'Unfortunately, not everyone thought that. Both sets of parents disapproved. My mother was nineteen when she had me; her parents weren't happy she didn't finish her degree. But they rallied round when I was born.'

'And your English grandparents?'

'My grandfather barely tolerated me, and he loathed my mother.'

'Why?' Kitty couldn't resist asking.

'Who knows? Because she wasn't English? Because she and my father defied him and got married? Because she was beautiful and loving? Because she bore a child with black hair instead of the Delfont blond?'

Kitty's heart ached for Sebastian as a little boy. She could just see him sitting here in the kitchen with his dark hair, his serious expression. He must have been very cute. 'But why take it out on you? You were just a child.'

'Not a good enough child to bear the name of Delfont, apparently. Grandfather was determined to turn me into a "proper English schoolboy".'

'How did he do that?'

'There were strings attached to any help from

my grandfather. Back then, Grandfather paid the first term of my father's university tuition—which would lead to a better job—on the proviso I came with him for the four months. Discipline at home and a private boys' day school, where I was miserable, was his tactic. He would have sent me away to boarding school, only my father refused to allow it.'

Kitty struggled to see why a grandfather would do that to a nine-year-old. 'I suppose you were in line to the title?'

'Third in line. I doubt at that stage he knew that my uncle Oliver was gay and had no intention of having children. Or if he did know, he refused to acknowledge it.'

'Your family story is…complicated.'

'You could say that, yes,' he said with a wry twist of his mouth.

'These are painful memories to revisit,' she said slowly, regretting that she had brought up the subject with her questions.

'Being back in this house has brought back memories. It seems like yesterday that I sat at this table—in this very chair—and snacked on treats Fran baked especially for me.'

'Did you see your mother during that four months?'

His face tightened. 'Only at half-term. But there were regular phone calls. A postcard every day. She painted each of them with a different little scene from her parents' house, where she was living. It was the only place I'd known that seemed like home.'

'But a poor substitute for your mum.'

'Yes,' he said tersely. He paused.

Kitty wanted to reach over the table and grip his hand hard. But she couldn't. It wouldn't be appropriate. The remembered bewilderment etched on his adult features was heart-wrenching. It brought back the agony of losing her parents when she'd been only fourteen and she couldn't bear to trigger it further, mixing it up with the more recent loss of her grandmother, the loss of the future she'd been so sure she'd have with Neil.

'I'm sorry,' she said, knowing how inadequate the words sounded, knowing there was worse to come in his personal story, with two generations of his family gone.

'It didn't last for ever. My grandfather's demands became unacceptable, as they always did. We went back home after I finished the term at school and my father his term at university. Life back in Spain went on much as before, only my father went back and forth to London to finish his teaching qualification. When I was eleven, an elderly uncle of my mother's died and the family allowed us to live in his run-down farmhouse and citrus orchard in Mallorca. My father got a position teaching in an English school for expats outside of Palma and I started school there. Later, they were able to buy the farmhouse.'

'The paintings in your library; are they—?'

'Of our farmhouse.'

'Painted by your mother?'

'In Mallorca, we lived not far from some popular tourist hotspots. She painted the local area because she loved it, but her art proved to be very appealing to tourists wanting to take home a tasteful souvenir. It became a steady income stream.'

'She was very talented.'

'In many ways. She painted those pictures in my library just for me. Mamá wanted me to never forget where I came from when I moved to London for university and to live with my uncle Oliver.'

'Yet you came from here too. Chelsea, I mean.'

'I never found it a conflict, until I ended up the heir.'

Kitty sensed there was a lot more underlying the flat statement than he had chosen to share. She ached to know more about this man, yet this wasn't the time to question him further.

'I can't begin to understand, and I'm sad if I've stirred up painful memories from a long time ago,' she said.

She felt utterly out of her depth with him. If the conversation swung around to the subsequent death of his parents and his uncle, she wouldn't know what to say, how to comfort him, if indeed he needed comforting, rather than stumbling into platitudes.

'You didn't stir up memories.' He indicated the room around them with a wave of his hand. 'The house did. But this room has only happy memories. And tonight has layered more on top of them.' He leaned towards her over the table. 'You're a wonderful listener, Kitty, and you don't judge. I don't know you very well at all, but it seems to me that you take people for who they are, and that's rare.'

She flushed, pleased by the compliment, not certain how to react. 'Thank you,' she said after a beat too long. 'But I've made some bad misjudgements of character along the way.'

He frowned. 'Don't blame yourself in any way for what happened with your boss. You expected him to behave as a manager working with young staff should and he broke that trust in a terrible way.'

'I only blame the people in that company who failed to protect me,' she said, looking down to avoid his too perceptive gaze.

'So you should,' he said. His voice hardened. 'And you know I believe you should have your revenge.'

'Vindication is what I want, not necessarily hardcore revenge,' she said.

And then there was Neil. But Kitty had no intention of sharing the story of that massive misjudgement with Sebastian. How could she have been so stupid as to trust in a future with Neil? The episode with the man she'd thought had loved her had scarred her. She could never again trust her judgement when it came to a man.

She got up from the table to clear the plates, putting up her hand to stop him from helping. 'Now we really need to get down to business.'

'Agreed,' he said with, she thought, a degree of reluctance.

She returned to the table with a takeaway box, which she placed between them, alongside two pretty china plates.

'There's a *torta caprese* waiting for us in there,' she said.

'What exactly is a *torta caprese?*' he said. 'You chose it.'

Kitty quoted in a theatrical style from the delivery description on the elegantly boxed dessert. 'Flourless chocolate almond cake, dusted with powdered sugar and served with macerated strawberries and mascarpone.'

'Sounds very good to me,' he said. 'What about we have the *torta* then get down to business?'

'Because before you get to taste dessert I'm going to torture you,' she said.

'Torture?' he said, humour and not one trace of alarm in his grey eyes.

'No cake until you've answered the first five questions on my list to help me brief Evelyn Lim tomorrow morning. I sense you've been avoiding this, even though it's the reason we're having dinner together.'

'Not fair,' he said. 'Totally unfair.'

'But necessary, yes?'

'Cake first would be better,' he grumbled.

Sebastian grumbled about the cake, but secretly he was tickled at how Kitty took charge to push forward his interests. Her chin was set at a stubborn tilt and yet she was charming in the way she manoeuvred him. He could see she would have been very good in her PR role.

'Okay,' he said, dragging out the word with mock reluctance.

'Question one: what colours do you like?' she said. 'If you opened your wardrobe door, what colours would you see?'

'I think you might know me well enough by now to know the answer to that,' he said. 'Want to hazard a guess?'

She tilted her head to one side and pretended to think. 'Let me see—how about black, black and black, charcoal, grey and perhaps a touch of white?'

'Close,' he said. 'It's easier for a man to get dressed if he doesn't have to worry about what goes with what.'

He wasn't being completely honest with her: wearing sombre colours suited his mood. There was colour in his wardrobe; he just hadn't chosen to wear it since his father's death had formed the first link in the chain of loss in his life.

'Shades of black and grey pretty much sum up the colours in your Dockside apartment. They worked well there.'

'But not here,' he said.

The undisguised look of relief on her face amused him. Had she seriously thought he would try to bring the minimalism of his apartment here?

'I'm glad you think so,' she said. 'Which brings me to my next question: what colours do you like for the house?'

'I don't like gloomy, but I don't mind dramatic.'

'A good answer for a designer, I would think. Any colour you particularly like?'

'Blue.' The colours of the sea and the sky in Mallorca, the mellow stone walls of the farmhouse, the citrus yellow of the lemons hanging from dark green leaves in the orchard. Those were the colours he loved but they were unique to his Spanish home. 'Muted tones of blue.'

'Any colour you don't like?'

'Mustard.' It was the first thing he thought of, to please Kitty with an answer. If the designer presented him with colours he didn't like, he would certainly let her know.

'How do you want the redesigned space to feel?' she asked. She wasn't taking notes, but he could see her mentally keeping track of his answers.

'Maintain the history of the house but make the rooms more welcoming.'

'Any rooms you particularly like or dislike the look of?'

'I don't actually dislike any room, just aspects of their décor. And I don't want my library changed at all. It's exactly how I want it.'

'Would it be safe to say the rooms where Lady Enid's influence is stronger are preferable to—'

'—the darker touch of my grandfather and possibly his grandfather? That's a given.' He looked at her across the table. 'And those are your five questions answered.'

'Please, just one more question,' she said, hands together in a gesture of mock pleading. 'It's an important one.'

How could he resist her?

'One more. Then cake,' he said darkly.

It wasn't that he was excessively hungry for dessert, but he was uncomfortable with answers about his private life that would be transmitted to a third person. He'd opened up to Kitty about his personal history because he trusted her and, for the first time, he wanted to share thoughts he had never shared with anyone else. She had a gift of making him feel comfortable with her, so much so he was starting to feel more at ease with himself and the forces that had shaped the last few years of his life.

'Final question,' she said. 'What's your budget for the designer?'

He made a dismissive gesture with his hands. 'Whatever she needs to spend to make the changes as quickly as possible.'

'I'll get Evelyn to give me a ballpark quote and you can look at that.'

'I'll authorise what you ask me to,' he said. 'But only the best quality.'

In truth, whatever the refurbishment cost, he could more than afford it. The penny-pinching days of his youth were long gone. He had independently amassed his own fortune, thanks to shrewd investments in biotech companies before they'd gone gangbusters, inheriting first from his father and then from his mother, including all ongoing royalties. Uncle Oliver had made him his heir, and his grandmother had left money from the trust fund she'd had from her wealthy family. Now the Delfont fortune and estates were in his hands, and with them the responsibility to maintain and improve them.

'I'll ask the designer to justify the costs,' said Kitty. 'Not that I think Evelyn would take advantage, but I think people work better within parameters.'

'You're the household manager,' he said.

'I'll always do my best for you, keep your interests first; you know that, don't you?' There was such honesty and sincerity in her blue eyes—blue was his favourite colour—he felt moved, grateful and humbled. She was an exceptional person in every way and he felt most fortunate to have her in his life, even if only temporarily.

'I do, and I'm grateful,' he said.

'And I'll bet you'll be even more grateful if I relent and serve the *torta*, with an extra helping of strawberries?'

'So you can read my mind now?'

'When it comes to dessert, it's not difficult to read you,' she said teasingly.

Could she also read that his interest in her was not just as a member of staff or a platonic friend? Or that he was finding it increasingly difficult to mask it?

CHAPTER EIGHT

THE FOLLOWING MORNING, the meeting with the interior designer went quite differently to what Kitty had expected. She'd been both surprised and disconcerted to see a very different Sebastian from the one with whom she'd shared confidences in the cosiness of the kitchen.

He'd greeted Evelyn Lim, a warm, confident woman in her mid-thirties, with polite professionalism but none of the enthusiasm that Kitty had expected from him for stage one of putting his stamp on the house. He'd reverted to that reticent, somewhat forbidding person she'd first encountered at the Docklands apartment and Kitty couldn't help but feel more than a touch intimidated.

He'd accompanied her and Evelyn on a perfunctory tour of the house, letting Kitty do most of the talking. At the end, he'd thanked Evelyn and told her that further communication should go through Kitty.

Kitty had taken Evelyn to Lady Enid's office,

where they'd discussed terms and timelines for Evelyn to present proposed schedules and Computer Assisted Design images. The first, most urgent priority was the dining room. Could Evelyn give it a new look by the time of the foundation dinner?

Kitty had apologised for Sebastian's aloofness. Evelyn had laughed off her concerns. According to the designer, Sir Sebastian was a mere two on a scale of ten for client grumpiness. 'I'm excited to be working with you again, Kitty, and on such a wonderful house,' she had said as they'd parted. Evelyn, more a work acquaintance than a friend, had stood by Kitty through the scandal, unfailing in her support.

Sebastian was tied up for the rest of the morning in meetings with his executive assistant, Guy. It wasn't until after the successful trial lunch with Alisa, one of the proposed job-share cooks, that Kitty was able to pin him down in his library.

The door was half open. 'Knock-knock,' she called out. Sebastian looked up from his desk, frowning at the interruption. She hesitated, not sure which Sebastian she was going to encounter. His frown turned to a welcoming smile and he stood up. 'Kitty. Come in.'

She realised she had been holding her breath and she let it out on a sigh of relief and an answering heartfelt smile. This was *her* Sebastian. She pulled herself up quickly. He wasn't her Sebastian;

in fact he didn't appear to be anyone's Sebastian. What she meant was this was the more relaxed Sebastian she had got used to. Not the distant Sebastian that Evelyn had met.

He gestured to the visitor's chair opposite his desk and sank back into his chair as Kitty took her place, putting the parcel she'd brought in with her on the floor by her side. She liked this room, with all the books and those beautiful paintings evocative of a happy time in a sunny climate. Now she knew their significance in Sebastian's life—and that they'd been painted by the person she knew as Marisol Matthew—she ached to look more closely at them. However, this room was not one she could just casually stroll in and out of. It was sacrosanct for Sebastian. She would have to brief whatever housekeeper they appointed on the importance of keeping his books and possessions exactly as he placed them. Hearing about his childhood yesterday made her appreciate his need for consistency and certainty—even if it could make people like her initially think he was being *difficult*.

'To what do I owe this pleasure?' he said.

'Good news. Evelyn has already come back to me with a few ideas for the dining room. She wants to know if you like the idea of switching out the heavy red for smoky blue which, in her designer's terminology, is "evocative and moody" while at the same time "serene". And she says it will work beautifully with the wood tones of the antique furniture and highlight the contrasting rich reds in that magnificent Persian carpet.'

'What do you think?' he asked.

Kitty appreciated the way he valued her opinion. Her confidence had taken a battering at Blaine and Ball.

'It sounds lovely to me,' she said. 'If you agree to the colour, Evelyn will send preliminary designs in the morning. Because she had a team of trades people ready to go on the other house, as soon as you approve her plans they can start on preparation. She says it's a blessing the room is painted, not wallpapered so they don't have to strip it and that the plasterwork is in such excellent condition.'

'Do it,' he said. 'I liked Evelyn, liked the examples of her work she showed us. Smoky blue sounds good to me and I know her CAD images will show me exactly how the room will look. I intend to be more involved with the master bedroom because that will be my personal space.'

'You didn't have many questions for Evelyn this morning,' Kitty said, making it an observation, not an accusation.

'I'm not good on things like that, especially with people I don't know. It's why I have you to organise them for me.'

'Yes, of course,' she said, biting down on a *yes but*. This renovation would take a lot longer than the six weeks she was contracted to work here. Who would provide the continuity?

He leaned towards her over the desk. 'Remember, you had the information about my preferences that you extracted under torture.'

He said it so seriously that she couldn't help but laugh. 'The torture of withholding *torta caprese*?' she managed to get out between splutters of laughter.

'You called it torture and the pain was very real,' he said deadpan. He cast a stern look at her. Then spoiled the effect by laughing too. His laugh was deep and rich and very engaging.

Laughing with her boss. This was nice. *Too nice.*

Laughter brightened his grey eyes, erased the tension from his face, magnified the power of his smile a thousandfold. Sebastian laughing was a different person yet again. She couldn't keep her eyes off him. It was as if his laughter had blown open a set of formidably high gates to reveal tantalising pathways she had never imagined: exciting, crazy—but still impossible.

The danger to her was that his laughter stirred not only desire but affection. It would be too easy to grow to care for Sir Sebastian Delfont. But nothing had changed to allow her to entertain the thought of anything that extended, even slightly, into a kind of friendship she doubted would outlast her six-week contract.

'I make no apology for my very effective method of torture,' she said. She willed her imagination to cease with the forbidden thoughts of other ways she would like to tease and tantalise him.

Sebastian sobered and Kitty took a deep breath to force herself back into business mode.

'Seriously, Kitty, your methods work,' he said. 'Briefing Evelyn Lim to get the dining room refurbishment started, organising that excellent lunch served by the first half of the job share team—you've again exceeded my expectations. You're quite the miracle-worker with all you've achieved already here.'

'No miracles involved,' she said with a shrug. 'It's amazing what a great address and a generous budget can do.'

'I think you underestimate your powers,' he said. Their gazes met for a long moment. She couldn't be sure what she read there—gratitude for sure, admiration too, and something else that evaded her. It flustered her and consequently she spoke too quickly, determined to change the subject.

'Speaking of powers, I'm not so sure about this one but we won't know until we try it,' she said. She reached down for the package and put it on the desk in front of her. 'This is the fun part of the day's agenda.'

'What's in there?' he asked.

'A smudging kit. I ordered it online and it just arrived.'

'You need a kit? I thought you burned a bunch of sage from the supermarket and waved it around the room.'

'I thought that too, but apparently not,' she said. 'Smudging is a serious business, apparently not to be undertaken on the spur of the moment. It seems you have to weave the leaves into a tight bunch and let them dry out for at least a week. If we want to smudge before we start the renovations, we don't have time for that.'

'Good point,' he said. He had surprised her with his willingness to try the ritual and she watched him closely for signs he might be making fun of her. But he seemed genuinely involved.

'Traditionally you also need an abalone shell and a large feather,' she said. 'Heaven knows where I'd find those myself. It seemed easier to buy a kit that included everything. The kit also includes instructions on how to conduct the smudging ceremony. There are an awful lot of reminders not to set the house on fire.'

'That's another good point. Should I be concerned about safety?' he asked. 'I don't want to risk burning the house down.'

Sebastian watched Kitty as she sought the right answer, her brow pleated in a slight frown. He liked the way she took this seriously, her sincere belief she was helping him to banish shadows from the past.

'No need for concern if we use care and common sense,' she said, rather primly he thought. Prim looked cute on her. Hell, any expression looked cute on her.

'You know I'm not so sure where common sense comes in when it comes to a smudging ceremony,' he said ruefully.

'Perhaps more a suspension of disbelief is required?' she said.

'That sounds about right,' he said.

'From what I read, smudging rituals originated in indigenous cultures around the world. If people have believed for a very long time that the ceremony banishes bad energy, maybe there's something to it. Even if it's just superstition it's worth a try. That is, if you can live with superstition.'

Sebastian snorted. 'Superstition was part of my life growing up with my Spanish family. My great-grandmother had a potted cactus on every entrance to her house to ward off evil. And no one would ever dare take off their hat and put it on a bed as that brought bad luck.' He thought about sharing with Kitty his *abuela*'s theory about a curse on the family and decided that would be going too far.

'Really? My grandfather blames his broken leg on the fact he absentmindedly walked under the ladder before he climbed it. And he would never open an umbrella inside the house.' Kitty rolled her eyes as she said it, which made Sebastian smile.

'And we're about to perform a smudging ceremony,' he said. 'I wonder what your grandfather would say about that.'

'I think he'd say it was very un-British,' she said. 'But each to his own, as my gran used to say. When do you want to start?'

'No time like the present, as my father used to say.'

'I'm okay with that,' she said. 'What about Guy? Do you want to involve him?'

'Absolutely not,' he said. 'Guy is out for the rest of the day.' He suspected his executive assistant would ridicule the idea, and therefore Kitty, and he couldn't allow that.

'It's just us then,' she said.

'Yes,' he agreed.

He liked it being just the two of them, knowing he could be himself with her. When the house was up and running, filled with staff, it would be very different. His spirits plummeted when he realised that by the time the staff were in place, Kitty would be back working in her own business. But that was five and a half weeks away and that was surely enough time to get to know Kitty, to see if his attraction to her had staying power, and to gauge if she had any interest in him.

'So we're smudging conspirators, and we won't

let anyone else into our secret circle,' she said, her eyes dancing with mischief.

'That's us,' he replied, surprised at how much the idea of a secret circle with just him and Kitty in it appealed.

She stood up. 'I'm dying to see what's inside the kit.'

Sebastian walked around to her side of his desk to join her. Considering her history, he stayed a respectful distance from her, although he was very aware of her sweet floral scent. He watched, bemused, as she opened the package with all the excitement of it being a gift.

She tore away the brown paper wrapping to reveal a brown cardboard box filled with a ten-centimetre bundle of dried leaves tied with white string, an iridescent abalone shell and a large feather in shades of brown.

'Interesting,' he said. 'Not quite what I expected.'

'Me neither. I think of sage leaves as green. This is white sage.'

Kitty pulled out a printed instruction sheet. 'We need to light the smudge stick then waft the smoke around the room with the feather. The resulting smoke is said to banish malignant energy from the house and invite good energy in. That means opening a window wide to avoid a traffic jam of conflicting energies.' She smiled. 'Who knew?'

She was delightful, and Sebastian found himself getting totally caught up in the game.

'Malignant energy? That's one way of describing my grandfather.' He glanced at his watch. 'Shall we get started?'

'First stop Sir Cyril's study?'

'Yes,' he said, keen to get on with it, surprised she knew that was the room most imbued with his grandfather's presence.

He followed Kitty down the stairs to the ground floor, admiring her back view, the sway of her hips in narrow-legged black trousers and a fitted jacket. Every time he saw her, he was struck again by how lovely she was. And each meeting left him both liking and admiring her more.

He stood outside the closed door, his hand poised above the handle. Kitty turned to him. 'You're having to brace yourself to go in, aren't you?'

He nodded, unable to speak, to admit even to himself that, after all these years, he still felt the fear. But Kitty understood; he knew she did without any words being exchanged. He wanted to reach out and hold her hand but he couldn't—and not just because she was holding the smudging kit.

'I used to feel physically ill when I got the summons to come to this study.'

'Let me go in first,' she said.

'No. I have to do it,' he replied as he reluctantly turned the handle and pushed open the door.

It was just a room, empty of the glowering figure of his grandfather, who had summoned him there on so many occasions to berate and lecture him, not just as a child but on those occasions he'd been obliged to see him as a teenager and as an adult. And yet a shiver ran down his spine at the memories that assaulted him.

Without a word, Kitty put the smudging kit down on the big traditional walnut desk. She went over to the windows and pulled the heavy ruby-coloured velvet curtains aside so light streamed into the room, dust motes dancing in a sunbeam. She pushed up one of the windows, enough for fresh air to come in. It ruffled the papers stacked on the desk and lifted the hair away from Kitty's face in fine blonde strands.

She turned back to him. Her eyes warm with compassion—and not a trace of the pity he would have hated—she put her hand on his arm. It was the first time she had touched him.

'When you were a little boy, was there physical abuse?'

He shook his head. 'Not…not sexual. No. Not physical either. He couldn't have hidden that from my father. More than once he told me how he'd like to take his belt to me, but the worst he did was what he called a "clip around the ears" which was basically hitting me on the side of the head.'

'What's that if not abuse?' Kitty flushed with outrage on his behalf.

'I suppose he did it to keep my father and uncle

in line, so perhaps it was seen as normal in this family.'

'Normal,' she muttered. 'I don't think so.'

'Relentless mental abuse was Sir Cyril's thing, about how useless I was, how stupid I was—because sometimes I forgot and spoke in Spanish—how I had to obey him in everything or my parents would suffer.'

'How would they suffer?'

'Probably withdrawal of funds. But at nine years old I didn't question what would happen to them as a result of my misbehaviour. I just wanted to protect them.'

Kitty cursed. 'I'm just so furious on your behalf. He sounds like a monster. How dare that man use his power and his money to intimidate a child?' She stopped. 'I'm sorry. It's not my place to—'

'Say anything you want. I appreciate your indignation.'

'Now I think I know why...' Her voice trickled away.

'Why what?'

'No. I shouldn't say—'

'Please say it.'

'Well, the reason you're not delirious with joy at inheriting all this. And...and the title. I... I'd wondered.'

He sighed. 'And yet it seems so ungrateful. Now you know what I mean when I say I feel like an imposter.'

'How can you say that? I mean apart from the obvious, that you…well, you look and act the part. But you're going to continue to do good, stepping into the shoes of Lady Enid.'

'As she had a fondness for teetering high heels, perhaps not literally.'

She looked up at him and his heart swelled at the compassion and understanding he saw there. 'I don't know you well, but I believe you're a good man doing your best to honour your legacy and to fulfil the wishes of your grandmother.'

'Thank you,' he choked out. There was a very long beat of silence as he looked into her face, so close, already so familiar. 'Your faith in me means a lot.' She bowed her head in acknowledgement and he wondered if he had given too much away about how he felt about his household manager.

Kitty dropped her hand from his arm and he felt immediately bereft of its warmth. She took a step back.

'Let's start the smudging,' she said briskly. 'We'll give your grandfather—or the memories of him—a proverbial clip around the ear and send his presence packing from this room.'

'I like the way you put that.' Sebastian picked up the smudging stick and held it out in front of him. He could imagine the horror with which his ultra-conservative grandfather would have viewed such a ritual taking place in his traditional study.

'Let me light it,' Kitty said, pulling a lighter

from her pocket. 'I found this in Lady Enid's desk. The sage stick is not meant to flame, just smoulder. When ash forms, we knock it into the shell. To get things happening, we wave the stick in an anti-clockwise direction and chant a mantra.'

'A mantra? You didn't prepare me for that.'

'I only just read it in the instructions,' she said. 'They give an example: "cleanse my home of negativity". But I think we can do better than that.' She looked up at him. 'Why not say to your grandfather what you were too scared, and under his thumb, to say when you were nine years old and powerless?'

'I don't think that will be difficult,' he said. He started to wave the smudging stick around in the requisite clockwise direction. It was a large room and it took a few waves of the stick for the pungent smoke to be noticed.

Kitty sneezed.

'Shall I stop?' he asked.

'No, I'm fine. Just getting used to the smoke. Start with your mantra.'

'Banish Sir Cyril's cruel words that linger in this room,' he intoned.

Kitty repeated his words very solemnly then paused. 'That's good. But I'm not sure it's what a nine-year-old would say.'

'How about goodbye, Grandfather?' he said.

'Grandfather begone,' Kitty intoned dramatically.

Sebastian emulated her theatrical tone. 'Get lost, Grandfather. Good riddance, Grandfather.'

'I like that,' she said.

He stopped himself. 'I'd better leave it at that before I embellish my mantra with words my nine-year-old self most certainly didn't know.' But he silently uttered those curse words under his breath, giving a private vent to his anger against the man who had caused so much heartache for his family.

Kitty looked up at him and he could see she was struggling not to laugh. 'I'm not laughing at you but at the thought of you as a sweet little boy standing up to your horrid grandfather and telling him where to go, with him unable to do anything about it.'

Sebastian joined in with her laughter. 'Sir Cyril would have absolutely hated this. He'd be incandescent with rage. I'm a naughty, defiant little boy, giving him the finger.'

'Like you never dared to do before. How does that feel?'

'Wonderful. Cathartic. Healing.' He placed the still smouldering stick carefully onto the shell. 'So much so I don't see the need to smudge any other rooms.'

'I'm so glad to hear that,' she said. 'Not about the smudging—I'm prepared to do every room if it helps—but that you feel so good about what we've done.'

Was it their combined laughter that made the atmosphere in the room seem to lighten? The symbolism of the smudging ceremony? The catharsis of chanting the mantras? The actual smoke itself?

It was Kitty. Her kindness, her belief in him, her sunshine banishing the shadows. *Kitty.*

'I really think he's gone from this room,' he said. 'And it's all thanks to you.' Without thinking about it, he swept her into a hug. Initially stiff with surprise, she then relaxed into his arms.

She felt so good there and for a moment he allowed himself to enjoy the comfort of her closeness, her warmth, the sweet scent of her perfume. Until he remembered the promise he'd made to her: *I will never step over the line of what is appropriate between employer and employee.*

Abruptly, he let her go, took a step back. 'I'm sorry. That shouldn't have happened.'

She looked up at him, her eyes wide. 'It's fine. Really.'

Tension hummed between them and he cursed himself for stepping over that line and changing the easy camaraderie they'd shared.

Until she sneezed again—once, twice, three times, little sneezes as cute and feminine as she was. She looked up at him, dismayed. 'I think I'm allergic to smudging.' She laughed again and after a moment's hesitation he joined in with her laughter.

He realised he hadn't laughed as much in years.

CHAPTER NINE

'KITTY, I'D LIKE you to act as my hostess for the Lady Enid foundation dinner party next Saturday night.' Sebastian's request came quite out of the blue. Kitty stared at him, totally taken aback.

She and Sebastian had just finished a gourmet lunch cooked by Josie, the second cook in the job share, and served to them in the breakfast room with its olive-green wallpaper and ornate carved sideboard. Sebastian's assistant, Guy, had been with them, but had just headed back upstairs. The crew working on the redecoration of the dining room had stopped for lunch too, downstairs in the kitchen, so it was a rare quiet moment on the ground floor.

'What exactly do you mean?' Kitty asked. But she didn't wait for an answer, rather launched into a list of what she'd arranged for the dinner. 'I've already organised everything. The menu has been chosen—and approved by you. Both the cooks, Alisa and Josie, will be on board for the evening. We raided your grandfather's cellar and found some remarkable wine. Waiters have been hired. Guy has had acceptances from all on the guest list and we've worked together on your speech. I've got Evelyn involved in the table decoration. We discovered a treasure trove of china, silver and crystal, not to mention antique table linen—your ancestors had fabulous taste. The most fashionable florist in London is on board. It was short notice, but I managed to pull strings as I used to work on their PR account. The room will be breathtaking.' Kitty knew she was blabbering on to the point of feeling breathless, but she didn't want to have to face answering his question.

Until she had to.

When her words finally petered out, Sebastian spoke in a low but firm voice from the other side of the table. 'By acting as my hostess, I meant for you to be by my side while greeting the guests and during the meal. There will be five people who were appointed by my grandparents to the board of the foundation and their spouses. They know nothing about me. I doubt they even knew Lady Enid and Sir Cyril had a grandson or, if they did know, I wasn't to be mentioned. There won't be one familiar face. My grandmother was concerned her foundation would struggle without her and these people hold the key to discovering if that's happened.' He paused. 'I'm dreading it. Please, Kitty, be there for me.'

Again Kitty was struck by that vulnerability

behind his good looks and title. Her immediate instinct was to help him. Now that she knew something of his background, she was beginning to understand him. She'd felt so close to him during the smudging ceremony. But that didn't mean she wanted to expose her own vulnerabilities, still raw after two years.

'Why me?'

'Because I'll feel comfortable having you by my side. I'm not great with people I don't know, nor the social chit-chat this kind of gathering requires.'

She had fantasised about him asking her out on a date and he'd asked her to be his housekeeper. Where was this request leading to?

'Don't you know someone else who could act as hostess for you? A date, I mean.'

'No. I haven't dated anyone since I broke off my engagement two years ago.'

'You were engaged?'

'It didn't work out,' he said shortly.

Despite her resolve, Kitty's heart did a flip at the confirmation he was single. She didn't realise how possessive she had become about him until she imagined him with another woman. She wondered what was behind the broken engagement, had to bite her tongue to stop her from asking for the details.

'Could you ask a friend to act as hostess?' she said.

Sebastian shook his head. 'I don't want to give

anyone the wrong idea that I want to get serious with them.'

How did she fit into that scenario? Kitty wondered. The *downstairs* being elevated to the *upstairs* for one night? Wasn't there a story about a girl like that? What was her name? Something beginning with 'C'. Got it—Cinderella.

'I honestly don't know what I can bring to the table for you, so to speak,' she said.

'You're warm, open, smart; you'll charm everyone.'

'That's nice of you to say so.'

Kitty couldn't help but feel flattered by his comment. However, she was a lot less warm and open than she used to be—she'd had to become more cautious, wary of other people. She'd been stung by those who'd appeared to have her interests at heart. And she wasn't at all sure that appearing as Sir Sebastian Delfont's hostess at a dinner party was a wise move.

'There's also the fact you're a PR professional,' he said. 'I feel confident you'll know exactly what to say.'

So not quite Cinderella, she thought. Not anything resembling a date, more along the lines of her being capable and useful—which was why she was here, she reminded herself. No need to feel disappointed that there wasn't something more personal behind his request.

'If—and I'm only saying *if*—I were to agree,

I'd be putting myself in the spotlight again by sitting alongside Sir Sebastian Delfont as his hostess at a private dinner party. What if someone recognises me?'

'You've seen the guest list. Is there anyone on it you know?'

'Not one.'

'If it's any consolation, I don't know them either,' he said with a wry twist of his mouth. 'But they're all well acquainted with each other.'

For a long moment her gaze met his as they shared a moment of connection. He was shy, she realised. Even though he was born into the elite strata of people who existed way above the A-list.

'Do you think they'll be like your grandfather, judging you, watching for you to put a foot wrong?'

'Something like that,' he said.

'You've got the power, you know. You've got the title, the wealth, the property that puts you, fair and square, on their level—even a step up from their level.' Not to mention the extraordinary good looks of a hero from one of his mother's books.

Sebastian got up from the table. Paced back and forth before stopping opposite her. 'Do you think I care about that? To be judged for what I own, rather than who I am?'

He towered above her and she got up from her chair to face him on a more equal footing. Not that he intimidated her. In fact she felt safe with him, never more so than in that brief, awkward hug they'd shared on the day of the smudging ceremony. She'd relived that hug several times in her mind and that feeling of safety seemed just as memorable as the soaring excitement of being so close to him.

'I haven't known you for long, but you don't seem to care about that at all,' she said. 'But, no matter who these people are, they've come into your orbit because they're actively working for charity by being on the board of your grandmother's foundation. That's a point in their favour, if you ask me. I suggest you give them the benefit of the doubt before you meet them.'

Sebastian looked at her for a long moment. He nodded and she could almost see the trepidation about the dinner lift from his face. 'Perfectly put, Kitty Clements. Of course you're right And that's why I need you by my side.'

'I couldn't bear any more media attention,' she said. She realised she was wringing her hands and put them behind her back. 'It was a nightmare in so many ways. What if the press got hold of it and decided to make more of it than your household manager helping you out for the evening?'

Her critics had accused her of 'punching above her weight' with regard to her much older boss and her so-called infatuation with him. The scorn they'd pour on her for 'aspiring' to a man with a title, even more 'out of her league' didn't bear thinking about.

'The dinner is in the privacy of my home, and the guests are unlikely to be seeking out scandal. Besides, you look different from the press photos. Your hair is much longer. And you're Kitty, not Kathryn. Do you have a second name?'

'Rose—my middle name is Rose.'

'I could introduce you as Kitty Rose, without having to lie.'

'How would you explain my presence? I can assure you people will be curious about any woman seen by your side.'

'I'd say you were a friend. We're heading that way, aren't we?'

She paused. There had been a relaxing of limitations since the smudging ceremony three days ago, although she didn't let herself think beyond that and had steered clear of any cosy dinners for two in the kitchen. 'Yes.'

'I'm asking you as a friend as well as an employee.'

Still she wavered. 'I'm not sure.'

'You're the only person I trust to be there for me,' he said stubbornly.

She sighed. 'How can I say no, when you ask me in that way?'

He didn't try to mask the relief in his eyes. 'Kitty. Thank you. Perhaps I can start to look forward to my debut entertaining event if I know you'll be there with me. There's a lot riding on it in terms of the future of my grandmother's foundation.'

'I've agreed to be your hostess, but let me make it clear I'm still not sure it's a good idea.'

For him perhaps, but not for her. She was way too attracted to him to be able to kid herself she wanted to be 'just friends' even if that were a real possibility. She didn't have erotic fantasies about men who were 'just friends'. Nor did her heart skip a beat when they smiled at her.

And that was apart from the risk of putting herself in the public eye again. But she had advised Sebastian to think positively; perhaps she needed to do so herself. Knowing the parameters, that being his hostess meant no more than an extension of her household manager role, she should let herself look forward to the dinner. After all, she'd organised the whole event and it was promising to be an exceptional evening.

Now there was just one more item to organise for the dinner party: something for her to wear. She was planning to meet Claudia the next day, Saturday. It could become a shopping day in Chelsea.

The Kings Road was lined with shops, even more in the Duke of York Square and heading up Sloane Street all the way up to Knightsbridge, home to Harrods and Selfridges. Some of the boutiques were press-her-nose-to-the-window only, the prices were so stratospheric. But there were also branches of popular fashion chains that were more in line with her budget, not to mention the Peter Jones department store in Sloane Square.

She planned to spend time on Sunday with Gramps in the rehab hospital and could swing by his house to pick up shoes and accessories on her visit to Gramps's house. It was a long time since she'd had the occasion to dress up. *To dress up for Sebastian.* She forced the insidious thought from her mind. Why would he care what she looked like?

CHAPTER TEN

ON THE EVENING of the dinner party, Sebastian thought it looked as if a magic wand had been waved around the dining room and completely transformed it. Evelyn and her team had indeed performed a kind of magic to get it looking like this in two weeks, all thanks to Kitty.

Gone was the deep red he had found so oppressive, replaced by smoky blue in varying tones with ivory highlights. The room still looked opulent and traditional but in a softer, more inviting way. The new curtains had formal swags and tails but in two shades of smoky blue in a lustrous silk, rather than the dark red velvet with tarnished gold fringing they had replaced. Lush flower arrangements, formal yet not stiff, were artfully placed as centrepieces on the table, the marble mantelpiece and on the pedestals that had always stood empty in his grandfather's day. The table was laid with vintage linen, white porcelain rimmed with silver, heirloom crystal and antique silver cutlery engraved with the Delfont crest. The silver and crystal glittered and gleamed under the light of the chandeliers.

There was a definite feminine touch present, yet it was a room where he felt immediately comfortable. For the first time he felt as though this grand old house could become his home.

Sebastian took a deep sigh of relief mingled with anticipation. The room was like a stage set, awaiting the actors to bring it to life. No one would do that better than Kitty.

He glanced down at his watch. Kitty should be here by now. He'd asked her to come downstairs in plenty of time before the guests arrived. Perhaps he should go up and escort her down on his arm, start the evening the way he intended to continue, with Kitty by his side.

He knocked on her door. 'Kitty, it's Sebastian,' he called, after he didn't get an immediate response. Still no answer. He was surprised, as Kitty was usually so punctual. He knocked again. Slowly the door opened.

'Sebastian, I... I didn't expect to see you. Aren't you meant to be downstairs waiting for your guests?'

'Aren't you meant to be downstairs waiting with me?'

Kitty was wearing a silky wrap in the style of a Japanese kimono, in a soft pastel aqua patterned with flowers. Not that Sebastian was overly noticing the pattern; his eyes were drawn to the way it gaped at the neck to reveal the edge of a lacy blue bra and the swell of creamy breasts. Kitty clutched the edges together to bunch the fabric and protect her modesty. He noticed her hands weren't steady. Why wasn't she dressed?

The silence between them became uncomfortable, until she raised her eyes to his. 'I... I can't do this, Sebastian. I was about to call you. I'm sorry.' Her eyes were huge, her mouth trembled.

'Do what? I'm not sure what you mean.' Could she not work for him any longer? Fear clawed him at the thought.

'The dinner. I thought I could be your hostess, but I can't. I... I'm too scared to face those people. I'm not just terrified of being exposed but also... I don't want to...to see you drawn into my scandal. This dinner event is important to you, and I don't want to ruin it.'

Sebastian was disappointed. Deeply disappointed. The thought of having Kitty by his side had made the prospect of meeting the trustees and their spouses so much less confronting. But at the same time he was stunned to see confident, capable Kitty reduced to this because of him. He knew she'd had doubts about the dinner but he'd still talked her into it. Because he needed someone to help him face up to his own fears. But that shouldn't be at a cost to her.

'Kitty, I'm sorry. I should never have asked you to step so far out of your comfort zone.'

She shook her head. 'No need to apologise. It made sense to ask me to hostess. It…it's just me—my fears, my doubts. Letting panic get the better of me. I didn't sleep last night for worrying. I'm the one who should be apologising for letting you down.'

She was wearing more make-up than usual, the dark shadowing around her eyes and the deep pink lipstick making her appear more sophisticated, and her hair fell to her shoulders in sleek waves, perhaps as a result of a visit to a hairdresser. It told him that at some point quite recently she had been committed to the evening.

He drew a deep breath, conscious he had to say the right thing and not make her feel worse, aware he was responsible for throwing her into the situation that was causing her this angst. 'You wouldn't be letting me down,' he said.

She started to protest but he put up his hand to stop her. 'I won't lie and say I'm not disappointed, but I understand. What the press did to you was appalling and even though I rate at practically zero the chance of them finding out about your presence at this dinner tonight, I totally get why you don't want to risk it. But don't worry about my reputation. The media have no power over me whatsoever.'

With his birthright and his fortune as protection, it would be difficult for the gutter press to come up with anything to attack him that would wound. But hurting Kitty was another matter altogether. He'd been sickened about some of their speculations about her motives. Her fears were well founded. Much as he wanted her at the dinner, he wouldn't try and guilt her into it.

'You're so kind,' she said, a tremor in her voice. 'Thank you for being so understanding.'

'I won't say you won't be missed, because you will. But I owe you my thanks for the incredible job you've done in pulling everything together to make sure the dinner will be a success. I predict the guests will be talking about how different it is now from my grandparents' day—and it's all because of you.'

'Thank you,' she said. 'Event planning is part of what I do…what I did.' She fanned her hand in front of her face. 'Don't be so nice that you make me cry; it will ruin my make-up.'

'I don't want you to cry because I don't want you to be unhappy. But if you want to cry, go ahead and open the floodgates, because if you're up here by yourself watching television it probably doesn't matter if your make-up is ruined.'

She blinked, bewildered. 'No, I don't suppose it matters at all.' She smiled, a shaky smile that didn't reach the corners of her mouth. 'How silly of me.' She started to laugh but it was tinged with hysteria. 'How very silly of me.' Big tears welled up in her lovely blue eyes. 'I… I'm sorry, I…' Her face crumpled as she choked on a sob.

Sebastian only hesitated for a second before he pulled her close. If she resisted, he would immediately let her go. But as his arms went around her she relaxed against him. He held her tight, murmured a litany of soothing words, told her she was wonderful and how much he valued her and that it didn't matter if she wasn't at the dinner—well, it did because he would miss her—but he'd be okay on his own and he was sorry if he'd pushed her into something she wasn't ready for. He wanted to comfort her, soothe her, protect her—never allow anyone to hurt her. A rush of emotion swept through him. No woman had ever made him care like this.

When her sobs shuddered to a stop, he gently released her.

'Sebastian, I'm so s—'

'There is absolutely no need to say you're sorry. I pushed you too hard. End of story.'

He gently wiped a smear of dark make-up from under her eye with his thumb, before realising he had no right to perform such an intimate action and taking a step back in case she misinterpreted it.

'Oh, my gosh, my make-up.' Her hands flew to her face. 'Is it smeared all over your tuxedo?'

She checked the fabric of the bespoke jacket he'd had made for him at Uncle Olly's Savile Row tailor. Her action brought her close to him again, her scent sweet and heady, and he felt intoxicated by it, entranced by the light touch of her hands on the lapels of his jacket. He had to fight the urge to take her in his arms again, to suggest he also skip the dinner and stay up here with her.

'No lipstick or mascara seem to have migrated to your jacket, thank heaven,' she said. 'That would have been awkward to explain to your guests.'

'I'm sure they'd be too polite to mention it if they noticed.'

She fell silent for a long moment, her face woebegone. 'What will you tell them about why I'm not at the dinner?' she asked in a very small voice.

'That you fell ill and had to send your apologies.' He glanced down at his watch. 'And, speaking of guests, I need to head back downstairs for when they arrive. Will you be okay?'

'Yes, of course. Embarrassed about the way I behaved, but okay.'

'I'll instruct the cooks to send up some dinner for you.'

'That won't be necessary,' she protested.

'Of course it will,' he said. 'After all your planning of the menu, I expect you'd like to taste it.'

As he headed for the elevator he was aware of Kitty's gaze on him from her doorway and he kept his shoulders straight, his step determined. It was only when he was in the privacy of the elevator that he let himself slump. He'd made such a mistake with Kitty. Not in asking her to be his hostess, but by not asking her out on a straightforward date in the first place. This whole subterfuge about having her work for him as his household manager had blown up in his face. He wanted her by his side without having to spin stories and half lies.

He hadn't trusted the instant attraction portrayed in his mother's romance novels for the basis of a relationship. Especially not after the disaster of his infatuation with Lavinia. But these two weeks in Kitty's company had proved that the attraction he felt for her was real. Getting to know her had only made him like her more, *want her more*. However, instead of making it easier to establish a relationship, he had made it more difficult. Imagine how much simpler it would have been if he could have introduced Kitty as his girlfriend to his guests tonight? And if the press had got hold of their connection he would be there to protect and defend her.

But it was useless to castigate himself with a barrage of 'what ifs'. Because without Kitty's amazing organisational skills and her gold standard contacts book, the dinner tonight wouldn't be anywhere near as successful as it promised to be. Left to his own devices, he would have held the event in the untouched dining room, dark with memories of his grandfather's cruelty, ordered catering from heaven knew where, not given flowers or anything like that a thought. And if Kitty wasn't working here she'd be working all hours with PWP, and he might have only seen her for a few dates—that was if she'd agreed at all.

Still, he couldn't stop the old gloom from descending on him—he realised how few his dark moods had become since Kitty had brought her own brand of sunshine to Cheyne Walk.

The way it was panning out, the dinner would be a success and launch him into his new role as Sir Sebastian Delfont, upholder of the family traditions. But it would be a hollow triumph without Kitty by his side.

The guests would start arriving soon. He headed to the reception room where they would gather before going in to dinner. With no Kitty, he had to face up to the ordeal of enduring the evening on his own, although all she'd done in preparation would make it easier—she'd even put her PR skills to use for his speech.

Evelyn, the interior designer, had done her best in the limited time to make a few welcome changes to the reception room. Sebastian sat there in the lull before the guests would arrive to be greeted with cocktails, and went through the list on his phone. He'd compiled notes on all ten guests—including photos—with details on their family situations, personal history and role as a trustee of the foundation so he'd have some basis for conversation. He was just checking on the name of the third wife of a titan of business when there was a quiet knock on the door. He quickly switched off his phone and slid it into his inside jacket pocket. Someone must have arrived early and was being ushered through by the staff hired for the evening.

He rose from his chair and pasted a polite smile on his face. Only to have it freeze as he heard Kitty's familiar, 'Knock-knock.'

'Come in,' he said hoarsely.

Kitty. Kitty in an elegant navy dress that was long-sleeved and modest but hugged her shapely body and teased with discreet hints of creamy skin through dark lace that sparkled with tiny crystals around the neckline. Kitty walking towards him, tentative in high-heeled silver shoes that strapped around her ankles. Or perhaps her tentative steps had more to do with trepidation about what kind of reception she might receive.

'I wonder if you're still in need of a hostess,' she said, her voice not quite steady.

'Only one in particular,' he said, unable to keep his eyes off her, fisting his hands so he didn't reach out and touch her. Her hair was pulled back on one side from her face with a glittering comb, her make-up perfect again with no trace of tears. She looked absolutely beautiful.

'Kitty Rose, reporting for duty,' she said, a tremulous smile dancing around the corners of her mouth.

'Why?' he said.

'I realised I'd not only be letting you down,

but also letting myself down if I didn't stand by my word.'

Relief and elation lifted him right out of his gloom. Kitty was here—all was well.

'I'm grateful you came to that decision.' There was so much more he wanted to say but he couldn't find the words.

She stood very close, looking up at him. He saw something in her eyes he didn't recognise. She swayed towards him—was it the heels making her unsteady or an invitation? As she parted her lips, he lowered his head to kiss her, but his mouth had barely grazed hers when there was a discreet cough at the door.

'Your guests are arriving, sir.'

Sebastian cursed quietly under his breath at the interruption.

Kitty smiled ruefully and reached up to kiss him lightly on the cheek. 'Shall we go and face them?' she said, placing her hand in the crook of his elbow and taking her place by his side.

CHAPTER ELEVEN

KITTY SAT AT Sebastian's right hand throughout the dinner. This time it was her turn to feel like an imposter. She was acting as hostess under entirely false pretences. That was the place for the guest of honour. The rules of etiquette dictated that she, as hostess, sat at the opposite end of the table. But Sebastian had told her in no uncertain terms what he thought of the 'rules' as they applied to him, and had insisted she be placed next to him.

She was so very glad he had done so. If she'd been at the far end of the table from him, she would have been second-guessing every word she said. His presence so close by, the knowledge he was watching out for her, helped her relax and she found the guests weren't as intimidating as she'd feared. In fact, she was surprised to find how much she was enjoying the evening. Not to mention how incredibly pleased she was at how flawlessly the meal service went and how well received the menu.

Before the main course was served, Sebastian

stood to give his speech. He welcomed everyone to the first annual dinner without his grandmother and explained how he intended to take over her role as chairperson of the foundation that bore her name and continue her high standard of ethics. He asked the trustees to be frank with him about any troubles they might have encountered. Throughout his speech, he was confident and charming, with touches of dry humour. Kitty's heart swelled with pride. How could he ever consider himself a fraud?

He took his seat beside her to a smattering of applause. 'Well done, Sir Sebastian,' she murmured.

He took her hand and squeezed it in silent thanks. *Sebastian was holding her hand.* He was coming down from the high of a well-received speech, and probably didn't even notice he had held onto her hand for longer than required, but she noticed. Every nerve-ending in her body noticed the contact, innocent though it was. Did it mean anything? Did that almost kiss in the reception room mean anything? She honestly didn't know what to think.

He was still the one holding all the power. Tonight she really was in Cinderella territory. On Monday she'd be back hunting for prospective housekeepers and cleaners and gardeners. In another month she'd be back packing boxes for clients' house moves. While she loved PWP, and the self-employment opportunity it had given her and Claudia, Sebastian had given her different opportunities here.

He'd given her the chance to try out her management skills and to prove she was still every bit as good at event management as she'd been back in that former life when she'd been a rising star in the public relations world. It made her realise how much she'd missed the work that she'd believed to be her lifetime career.

And her attraction to him? It wasn't just sexual attraction she felt for Sebastian; the last two weeks had seen her liking him more each day. More than liking. But Sebastian was a man she couldn't have. They still came from very different worlds—nothing had changed there.

The more he took on the mantle of the Delfont title and fortune, the more he might become Sir Sebastian, the millionaire—or perhaps even billionaire for all she knew—welcomed by that top strata of society, and less the guy who would enjoy a meal in the kitchen with his household manager or laugh his way through a smudging ceremony. He said he didn't care if she dragged him into a scandal, but the more he became involved with the foundation, the less he might welcome adverse attention from the tabloids—and there was always the risk she would attract that, until she could clear her name.

She slipped her hand from Sebastian's as she

answered a question from the woman sitting next to him about the interior designer who had transformed the dining room. She wasn't the first person this evening she'd shared Evelyn's contact details with, and she was glad her amazing work here might lead to new commissions for her.

The trustees varied from middle-aged to elderly and all appeared pleased that Sebastian would be stepping into Lady Enid's shoes. So far, no one seemed to make any connection between Sebastian's friend Kitty Rose and the scandalous Kathryn Clements. They were too polite to grill her about her friendship with him and seemed happy to accept the explanation that they had met through work. Sebastian freely acknowledged her part in planning the dinner and she graciously accepted their praise, finding it just the teeniest bit difficult to keep a straight face. She'd planned functions like this before but she'd never attended as a guest, let alone as the hostess to a handsome man with a title. It all seemed surreal.

Sitting on her other side was a charming retired judge and his erudite professor wife. They confided that they had been close to Lady Enid—although not, it seemed, Sir Cyril. They'd become tight-lipped at any reference to Lady Enid's husband, without actually saying anything critical. The judge hinted that he wanted to retire from his role as trustee as he and his wife wanted to move permanently to their house in Portugal. That would give Sebastian the opportunity to appoint his own people to the board. Kitty would share that information with Sebastian at the end of the evening. It might be the first step to putting his stamp on another aspect of his inheritance. And a move further away from her.

After all the frantic planning to get the dinner organised it was over all too soon. After the farewells were made, Kitty stood facing Sebastian in the hallway after the last of his guests had left.

Behind closed doors, the dining room and kitchen were still a flurry of activity as the temporary staff cleared up. They'd be back in the morning to complete such tasks as polishing silver and putting everything away in pristine condition. One of the joys of being wealthy must surely be having someone to do all that for you, Kitty thought. Small scale dinner parties at her flat used to leave her facing a mess of unwashed dishes to clean up in the morning while—now she thought of it—Neil slept it off. Recently she'd heard he had announced his engagement. She'd waited for the rush of jealousy and pain, but it hadn't come. By his betrayal, her ex had killed all feeling she'd ever had for him. She couldn't find it in herself to wish him well, just felt a pang of pity for his fiancée.

Sebastian turned to face her. 'Thank you, Kitty. Thank you for everything you did to make the evening such a success.'

'It did go well, didn't it? I'm pleased. You could

reasonably expect something would go wrong, but nothing actually did. And didn't the room look beautiful? I kept looking around, hardly able to believe it was the same room we looked at just two weeks ago. The smoky blue made such a difference with the silver instead of the red and the gold.'

'As a strategy it also worked,' he said. 'It marked significant change.'

'You mean out with the old and in with the new?'

'Something like that. You certainly did me a favour finding Evelyn Lim.'

'I can't wait to see what she does with the rest of the rooms.'

Only Kitty probably wouldn't ever get to see those rooms finished. The master bedroom required major refurbishments and so did the bathrooms. That would take time, and her time here in Cheyne Walk was limited. She felt inexplicably sad about that, perhaps like Cinderella had felt at the prospect of returning to the ashes and dust of her downstairs life. She didn't want to face the thought that, like Cinderella, she would be mourning the loss of not the prince in her life but her baronet.

'Me too,' he said.

'It's getting late,' she said. 'I'll head upstairs.'

'I'm not tired. I'm still buzzing from the evening and not ready to turn in.'

'Me neither.' After the emotional ups and

downs of the day, and then being 'on' all evening, she was wide awake.

'Would you like to come for a walk with me?' he asked. 'Get some fresh air.'

'Now?'

'Why not?'

'Because I'm not used to walking the streets at night. I don't feel safe.' She didn't like to admit it; however, that was the way it was.

'You'd be with me. Would you feel safe then?'

She didn't hesitate. 'Yes.' On more than one level, she felt safe with Sebastian.

'It will be chilly out; I'll get your coat from the cupboard,' he said.

Kitty glanced down at her gorgeous new silver stilettoes. 'I'll pop upstairs and change into boots.'

Five minutes later, she caught her breath at the November chill as she stepped out of the front door and into the night.

'Cold?' Sebastian asked.

She wrapped her arms around herself. 'A little; it was so warm inside.' She needed to collect her warmer coat when she went home the next day.

'Here,' he said as he removed the cashmere scarf he was wearing. 'Wear this.'

'Oh, no, I couldn't—'

'Please, I don't need the scarf.'

He looped the soft grey scarf around her neck. His fingers, in their fine leather gloves, brushed her neck and sent shivers of awareness down her spine. He was close. Kissing distance close. They'd come so close to kissing earlier in the evening. Or had that just been relief on both their parts that she'd overcome her panic attack?

'Better?' he said. All the better for being so close to him. She wanted to reach up and bring his face down to hers, to finish the kiss that had been cut short before.

'Much better,' she said. She nestled into his scarf. It was warm and soft and carried a hint of his scent. 'You might not get it back,' she teased.

'It's yours,' he said.

'Oh, no, I didn't mean… I couldn't possibly accept it.'

'The scarf looks so much better on you than on me,' he said. 'I've got others.'

Of course she couldn't keep his scarf. But she was certainly going to enjoy wearing it tonight, and the heady sense of connection to him it gave her. She pulled it up higher over her ears.

'Where are we walking?'

'I usually cut through over there past the statue of St Thomas More to take us to Chelsea Embankment.'

'Then a walk by moonlight along the Thames,' she said.

She nearly added, *How romantic*, but stopped herself just in time. She couldn't let herself think there was anything romantic about a man and his household manager taking a stroll to wind down after an event that had been gruelling for both of them. *Except there had been that nearly kiss.*

It was quiet as they walked along the paved Embankment pathway, softly lit by a progression of traditional London lampposts placed along the river wall. There were trees still hanging onto some of their autumn leaves on the left, on their right the river at high tide, the occasional wash from passing boats surging against the wall. The night was crisp and clear with a full moon hanging in the sky. There weren't many people about, even though it was Saturday night, and not much traffic on the road or the river. It felt as if they had London all to themselves.

'It's magic,' she said. 'Even better than it is during the day. I've walked up here a few times, thinking I'd like to see the Chelsea Physic Garden.'

'I run here most mornings,' he said. 'Along the riverside pavement, across Chelsea Bridge to Battersea Park, then over the Albert Bridge and back home.'

What an incredible part of London to live in. She wondered if he would become complacent about the privilege; she doubted she ever would. Not for the first time she thanked her lucky stars for giving her the chance to stay here for six weeks, the opportunity of a lifetime.

'Impressive,' she said.

'Not really; it's less than two miles. But it wakes me up for the day.'

She could think of better ways to wake him up, she thought, glad he couldn't see her blush in the semi-darkness at another of those erotic fantasies about him that continued to plague her. It was entirely inappropriate, she knew, but she wanted him. Wanted him so badly he was beginning to invade her dreams. When she really thought about it—which she tried not to—she had wanted him from the day she'd first met him.

'You must get up very early.' He'd always been around, dressed for work, when she'd come downstairs at nine.

'I like the mornings,' he said.

She shuddered. 'I'm a night owl through and through. I can stay up all hours, but I hate getting up early in the morning. Like I'll have to do tomorrow.'

'Do you have something special planned for your day off?' he asked.

'Visiting my grandfather in the rehab hospital.' That really made her sound like a social butterfly, didn't it? 'He has friends from the village who visit but he needs to see me and…and I need to see him.'

'Of course you do. How do you get down to Kent as you don't have a car here?'

'The parking is way too expensive around here. I catch the train when I go back home. My car is parked there.'

'Can I drive you tomorrow?'

Kitty was too flabbergasted to answer. 'You mean to visit my grandfather? Why would you want to do that?'

'To help you out. To enjoy a day out of London. To meet your grandfather and talk to him about gardening. Have lunch together somewhere.'

'But why? I still don't get it.'

She scarcely noticed they'd stopped walking and stood near the river wall, facing each other.

'Because I want to get to know you better, Kitty.'

'But you already know me. I—'

He put his hands on her shoulders and looked into her face. Kitty stilled, uncertain of what was happening.

'I know you as an employee. I want to get to know you outside of a work situation.' His face was in shadow and she couldn't read his eyes. 'Would it be an intrusion for me to spend your day off with you tomorrow?'

'Oh,' was all she could manage to squeeze out with a voice that felt too constricted to form a proper word.

'Is that a yes or a no?'

There was an edge to his voice that made her realise that her answer was important to him.

'It's a *no*. I mean *no* to it being an intrusion, *yes* to spending the day with you.'

She sensed him relax at her answer. 'Good,' he

said gruffly. 'I understand why you're reluctant to be seen in public with me in London.'

His hands still rested lightly on her shoulders, which brought him close and gave a certain intimacy to the conversation.

'Visiting Gramps isn't going to be very exciting,' she said.

'The company is sure to be good. You, for a start, and I like the sound of your grandfather.'

'Are you serious? You really want to visit my grandfather? It's a small community hospital so isn't too grim, but it's still a hospital.'

'I'd be meeting someone who is important to you.'

'He certainly is that,' she said with a catch in her voice.

'I can wait outside while you visit, if you'd prefer,' Sebastian said.

'No, Gramps would want to meet you. He's heard about the work I'm doing for you and fascinated by me living in what he calls millionaires' row. He says it doesn't sound like you're too la-di-da about being a Sir and all that. He's very down-to-earth, my gramps.'

'I like the sound of him. And I'll try not to be too la-di-da.'

She smiled. Never had he sounded more posh.

'He's a good man,' she said. 'I think you'll like him.'

'If he's anything like you, I'm sure I will,'

Sebastian said. 'You know you're a very good woman, don't you, Kitty Clements?'

'I…er…well, I try.'

'You're kind, you're understanding and you're not judgemental. Do you know how rare that is?'

'Thank you,' was all she could manage to choke out in her surprise. She'd had no idea he'd been so observant of her. His words warmed her, but she didn't think she was rare at all. There must have been people in his life who had made him believe that, as well as his tyrant grandfather. But, for all the horrible people at Blaine and Ball, and the media people who had shredded her reputation, she firmly believed there were more good people than bad in the world. She was fortunate to have friends and family who had never doubted her.

'You've made what could have been a very difficult time for me less difficult,' he said. 'Not just the dinner tonight, which would have been far more of an ordeal without you, but the way you've smoothed my path ever since I moved into my grandfather's house.'

'Do you think you'll ever start to think of it as your own house?' she asked.

'I believe so, thanks entirely to you.'

'I'm flattered,' she said. 'And glad.'

She remembered how she'd feared he might be difficult, and instead it had turned out he wasn't difficult at all, and how much she enjoyed working with him. How some nights she lay awake in her bed on the top floor of the house and thought about him sleeping alone below, in the bedroom that had been his father's as a boy, and tried to keep at bay her fantasies of creeping down the stairs and knocking on his door.

'After we've visited your grandfather, we could have lunch in a pub or somewhere off the beaten track where there'd be little chance of you being recognised, or me for that matter,' he said.

'That rules out the one pub in Widefield, as all the locals know me. We'd be besieged. We'll have to go further afield.'

'I'm sure we'll find somewhere,' he said.

'There's a nice gastro-pub not too far from the hospital, on the river, good food. I could book online for lunch when we get back inside.'

'You're a marvel of efficiency as usual,' he said.

Efficient, capable, understanding. Was that the only way he saw her? For a painful moment she longed for him to see her as beautiful, exciting, sexy—the way she saw him in her fantasies.

She looked up at him, willing him to see her as something beyond his household manager, beyond a make-believe friend to act as his hostess. In the half-light his face was in shadow and his grey eyes seemed dark and unreadable. But there was a glimpse of something there that made her heart thump and her breath become shallow. Her gaze held his for a long moment. Then he lowered his head to hers. In silent assent, she raised her face to meet him then sighed into the pleasure of his kiss.

She wound her arms around his neck to bring him closer; he slid his hands to her waist. Even through her coat she could feel his warmth and strength. His kiss was gentle and she kissed him back, enjoying the tender touch of his mouth against hers, the slight rasp of his beard shadow against her face, pleasurable rather than painful.

Sir Sebastian was kissing her and she was kissing him back.

It was such a sweet kiss and she was loving it, but it wasn't enough and she ached for more. The signal would have to come from her. Aware of her history, he would be respectful of her and she appreciated that. She slipped her tongue between his lips in unspoken communication that she was happy to deepen the kiss.

He needed no urging. Lips and tongues became more demanding as the kiss quickly whooshed into something passionate and intense and urgent. She was stunned it escalated so fast from a tender exploratory kiss to something that had her pressing her body close to his, cursing their coats, their gloves, wishing she was alone in a bedroom— any room—with him instead of in a public place. Somewhere, anywhere where she could—

Bewildered, she broke away from Sebastian's kiss. A kiss that was so much more than something physically exciting and arousing. There was something deeper, more profound to it that stirred up emotions she had no right to be feeling. Emotions she couldn't handle right now.

He staggered and she had to put out her hand to steady him, glad of the contact, having felt bereft of his touch when she'd stepped back from him to break the kiss.

'That…that was a surprise,' he said.

'I… I wasn't expecting that,' she said at the same time, her hand still on his arm.

They stared at each other and even in the shadowed light she could see the same bewilderment and uncertainty on his face that he must surely see on hers.

'Wow,' he said.

'Double wow,' she said.

Then she started to laugh, with exhilaration and incredulity and a big dash of joy that she was still capable of feeling something so visceral and real.

Still looking dazed, he joined in her laughter. 'I… I had no idea.'

'It was just a kiss,' she said, spluttering with the remnants of her laughter.

Slowly, he shook his head. 'Oh, no, it was so much more than that.'

'Perhaps we've unleashed something that needs to be put on the back burner until after we stop working together,' she said, forcing the tremor from her voice. It was the only way she could quickly put into words her sudden urgent desire for distance and space so she could process what had just happened.

He put his arm around her. 'You could be right,' he said. 'C'mon, let's get home.'

His ancestral home—*her* temporary residence in the servants' quarters. She mustn't forget that. His arm rested companionably around her shoulder as they made their way back to the house on Cheyne Walk.

CHAPTER TWELVE

SEBASTIAN LOOKED AROUND the small, attractively furnished living room of Kitty's grandfather's house while Kitty was upstairs packing some clothes for both herself and her grandfather. He was hungry for details of her life and this room was rich with them.

Framed photos were everywhere: on the bookshelves, the mantelpiece, the coffee table. They tracked Kitty from a tiny baby, held proudly in the arms of beaming young parents, to a triumphant, laughing toddler walking on chubby legs towards her doting mother, to a posed professional group photo of Kitty with her parents and an older couple who must be the grandparents, the resemblance was so strong. In pride of place, hanging over the fireplace, was a large photo of Kitty at her university graduation, in cap and gown. There were pictures of her in school uniform through primary school to high school, with her arms around some girls in a netball team, snuggled with a golden Labrador, in a long gown beside an obviously besotted teenage boy at a school formal. And always Kitty with her parents, until they disappeared from the photos and there was a young teenage Kitty with sad eyes, obviously struggling to smile.

Sebastian's heart turned over for her. He had suffered loss, but he hadn't lost his parents until he was an adult. He looked more closely at the photos, saw the resemblance between Kitty, her mother—who hadn't been given the chance to grow old—and her grandmother, all attractive women with blonde hair and blue eyes, and variations of that same open warm smile. A beautiful family, struck by tragedy and yet uplifted by family loyalty and love.

On the bookshelves he noticed a row of Marisol Matthew books, picked one up and put it down again. He still missed her too much to open it and read his mother's words. Yet he marvelled at the legacy she'd left behind, a legacy that reached as far as this suburban living room and was a link to Kitty.

What would be his legacy? Increasing the already huge Delfont fortune? An image of a laughing little girl with dark hair and blue eyes running towards him flashed through his mind. A daughter? Since his broken engagement, he hadn't let himself think as far forward as having children. One day, perhaps, maybe. If ever he met the right woman, if ever she believed him to be the right man.

Lavinia had pressed for the idea of having a child as soon as they were married. But even before he'd become totally disillusioned with her, he'd realised she'd had an ulterior motive. His former fiancée had been aware that his uncle Oliver didn't want children and that ultimately Sebastian would inherit. Any children Lavinia might have borne him would have been in line to inherit the Delmont fortune, although only a son could inherit the title. Her interest in having children with him had been about securing her stake.

Her words still haunted him: *No woman will ever want to live with you.* Yet Kitty didn't seem to find his company too objectionable, and right from the get-go she'd been aware of his obsessive need to have his things in order that Lavinia had deemed so unacceptable.

Kitty. That kiss had changed everything. It had made him realise what might be, if he could overcome his lack of trust not just in others, but in himself. If he could let genuine feelings develop instead of constantly slamming the brakes on them. Looking at her family photos today had brought home the painful empty truth of his own life—the people closest to him whom he had loved and who had loved him had all died. He was fearful that if he dragged out from the depths of his heart the courage to love again, he would lose that love—and he didn't know if he could cope with more loss. Was that the curse his *abuela* feared?

He walked over to the glass doors that opened out to the narrow back garden. As with the front, it was immaculate. He didn't know what the plants were but there were masses of flowers in bloom, a small tree bright with autumnal orange leaves, a winding path of crazy paving leading right to a gate in the back fence. There was real talent in creating a garden as harmonious as this.

He sensed Kitty coming into the room—her footfall, her scent—before he turned to see her. He caught his breath at how lovely she looked, dressed casually in blue jeans, a fluffy powder blue sweater, short boots, her hair a golden mass around her shoulders. But when did she ever look less than lovely? She joined him at the doorway.

'Delightful, isn't it?' she said. 'Gramps is never happier than when he's pottering around in his garden. And there's more natural beauty behind the fence. The gate leads out to open fields. It's a wonderful place to walk, and it's covered in wild-flowers in the summer. Birdwatchers like it too.'

'This was a good place for you to live.'

'When my parents were alive we lived in Brom-ley, which isn't very far away…they were both schoolteachers. We visited my grandparents often, so it wasn't unfamiliar when I…when I had to move here to live with them.'

She turned away, hiding, he thought, remembered grief. The pain of losing beloved parents always stayed raw around the edges. She'd lost her grandmother recently too. And had also suffered a different kind of loss with her career, her lifestyle. She must have felt rudderless until she and Claudia had the initiative to set up their own business.

Kitty sneezed, that cute little sneeze that made him smile.

'Have you been smudging?' he asked.

She smiled. 'No need for that here. No malevolent spirits casting their shadows. The house was a new-build when my grandparents moved in. It's the dust from the bathroom renovation upstairs that's making me sneeze.'

'Let's get you outside, shall we?' he said, following her to the front door. 'Here, let me take that bag.'

'Gramps asked me to bring his best tweed jacket to wear for his meeting with you.'

'I'm honoured.'

'You should be. He was always a snazzy dresser, but hasn't bothered so much since Gran died. He said he only ever wanted to look his best for her.' Her voice was tinged with sadness.

'They were happily married?'

'Very much so. Gramps and Gran adored each other. They met each other at a dance when they were eighteen and that was it.' She paused. 'Somewhat like your parents, really.'

'No wonder your grandmother liked reading my mother's books.'

'I liked reading them too, although I sometimes wonder if they gave me unrealistic expectations.'

'Expectations?'

'About romantic love and honourable men.' Her mouth turned down in a bitter twist.

'You say that with a distinct air of disillusionment,' he said.

'Disillusionment? You could say that.'

'Who made you feel that way?'

'You don't want to know,' she said. 'He doesn't deserve airtime.'

Sebastian looked down into her face. 'But I do want to know; I want to know so much more about you. Last night. It seemed like it could be the start of something…something deeper between us.'

She looked up at him. 'Did you feel that too?'

He paused, not wanting to frighten her off by revealing the intensity of his feelings. 'To be put on hold, as you say.'

'Until we can meet each other as equals, not employer and employee.' She swept her hand around to indicate the house. 'Although my home is somewhat more humble than yours.'

He snorted. 'Humble? Your grandfather's house is a palace compared to our farmhouse in Mallorca when we first started living there. The old uncle, who had been there on his own, had let it practically fall down around his ears. He had chickens living in the house. I remember they were scratching around in the kitchen when we arrived. I was enchanted at the idea of them becoming my pets, maybe even sleeping in my room. My mother, needless to say, had no intention of allowing any such thing.'

'Seriously?'

'It's true. I didn't notice all that was wrong with the place. I just loved it that at last we had our own home.'

'What happened to the chickens?'

'The way my father told it, his first job at the new place was to build a chicken coop. In the meantime, the chickens roamed around outside during the day and slept in the decrepit laundry room, along with the goat.'

She laughed. 'It must have been heaven for a young boy.'

'Not so heavenly for my parents at first, but over the years they worked hard to turn it into the beautiful home it is today.'

'You must share that story with my grandfather; I think it would give him a good laugh,' Kitty said as they walked out of the door.

It wasn't until they were in his car and heading for the rehabilitation hospital that Sebastian realised Kitty hadn't told him anything about the man who had put such a bitter expression on her face.

* * *

Of all the places Kitty thought she'd see Sir Sebastian Delfont looking relaxed and happy, it wasn't the communal living room at the hospital where patients met their visiting family and friends.

After a brief initial awkwardness, Sebastian and Gramps had hit it off. So much so that she sat to the side as they talked, Sebastian with his tall frame folded onto a small plastic chair, Gramps with his left leg in a brace stretched out in front of him, his crutches resting against his larger, more comfortable chair. The leg had had to undergo surgery and a plate and pins inserted, and there was a lot of physical therapy still ahead of him. But Gramps wasn't talking about his injury. Rather he was telling Sebastian the story of how as a little boy he had been evacuated during World War Two from London to Widefield, where it was considered to be safer and less likely to be bombed.

Kitty never tired of hearing her grandfather's tale of how he—barely six years old—and his brother had been sent on a steam train to Widefield, with a small bag of possessions each and brown paper labels around their necks to identify them. How they'd been lined up with the other evacuee children to be billeted with a host family. He and his brother were one of the last to be chosen, fortunately by a kind older couple who'd welcomed them into their home for the duration of the war.

'Why did your parents allow that?' Sebastian asked Gramps. 'It must have been distressing for all of you.'

'To keep us safe from the bombing in London. The government called the mass evacuation of London's children Operation Pied Piper. My mother visited us as often as she could; my father was fighting in the Middle East. After the war ended, we'd come down here for holidays with my host family, who became like real family. When I grew up and could choose where I lived, I came back to Widefield and have never moved from here since.'

Sebastian turned to Kitty. 'Our generation has had it so easy by comparison.'

'You young people have your own stresses,' Gramps said. Sebastian's mobile phone rang. Gramps chuckled. 'Such as being at the beck and call of electronic devices.'

Sebastian excused himself and headed outside to take his call, which he said was important. Kitty watched him as he strode towards the door, admiring his rear view in black jeans with a hopeless kind of yearning.

'He's a good bloke, love,' Gramps said. 'You could do worse.'

'We're just friends,' Kitty protested. 'Not even that, really. He's my temporary boss.'

'Rubbish. I might be old but thankfully I'm not blind. I saw the way he looked at you, and you at him.'

There was something there, that extraordinary kiss had proved that, but it was too new and fragile to admit it to anyone—it was difficult enough to admit it to herself.

'I won't always be around to look after you, you know,' Gramps said.

Her heart chilled at the thought of losing her beloved grandfather. But they'd had this conversation before. 'I don't need a man to look after me, Gramps.'

'Yes, you do, and he needs someone to look after him. That's what it's all about, to look out for each other, be each other's best friend, be loyal and—above all—always be kind to one another.'

'That's your secret recipe for happiness?' she asked.

'It's not so secret. Your mother and father loved each other like that too.'

Why was she talking about commitment as if it were something possible with Sebastian? Because she wanted it. Wanted *him*. Not as her boss. Not as a friend. Not as a fling.

'But, Gramps, we come from such different worlds. You should see his house in London. He's wealthy almost beyond comprehension. He downplays it but he's a baronet. *Sir* Sebastian.'

'And you're a smart, well-educated young

woman the equal of anyone in Britain. For all his wealth and status, your Sebastian is just a man like the rest of us. To me he seems in need of someone loving and kind-hearted like you; there's a sadness at the core of him.'

'Do you think so?' Her grandfather sometimes astounded her with his shrewd insights.

'If you like him, don't let pride or self-doubt stand in your way. He's twice the man of *that* Neil.' Gramps hadn't liked Neil and always called him *that* Neil. Maybe she should listen to her grandfather when it came to Sebastian. Take the first step towards him. *If she dared.*

When Sebastian joined them again he tried to convince Gramps to come with him and Kitty to the riverside pub she'd booked for lunch, but he was adamant that his leg wasn't fit enough to be taken on an outing.

'Next time,' Sebastian said as he shook her grandfather's hand in farewell.

Next time?

'Talk about a tale of two grandfathers; how different could mine and yours possibly be?' Sebastian said, after they were settled back into his car. It wasn't the latest model of European sportscar, as she might have expected, but rather a meticulously restored British classic. He made no move to drive away and she welcomed the opportunity to talk with him.

'I really liked Stan,' he said.

'I could tell,' she said. She swallowed hard. *Take that first step.* 'Seeing you with him, listening to the way you talked about Mallorca, made me realise we have more in common than I ever could have anticipated.'

'Apart from the fact we both have books by Marisol Matthew on our bookshelves?'

'That too.'

'I told you I didn't always live in a mansion on Cheyne Walk, nor did I have aspirations to it.'

'The apartment in Docklands. That looked like a different kind of upscale lifestyle altogether.'

'The home of a man intent on making as much money as he could, as quickly as he could,' he said. 'A driven man.'

'A lonely man? It seemed, despite your artworks, to be an empty kind of place.'

'Perhaps it was, although to me it symbolised independence and freedom.'

'Tell me about your fiancée.'

'*Ex*-fiancée,' he corrected her. He paused. She noticed his fists were clenched. 'This is very difficult for me to talk about.'

'I appreciate that,' Kitty said. 'But I've been told I'm a good listener. And someone recently told me I wasn't judgemental.' That earned her a smile from him.

'Lavinia was bad news from the start, although I didn't realise that at the time.'

'We never do,' Kitty said.

'My uncle Oliver was very sociable and had a circle of friends who were always at his parties or at the theatre or a concert. I sometimes went along; his young nephew was somewhat of a novelty.'

His extremely handsome young nephew, Kitty thought.

'Lavinia was on the edge of the circle. She was older than me, gorgeous, very glamorous. She hooked me without too much trouble.'

His cynical tone surprised her. 'Hooked you?'

'I was what they called "a good catch". Everyone knew my uncle had made me his heir, and I wasn't exactly hard up in my own right. I fell hard for her. She supposedly fell for me. What I didn't know was that she was the long-term mistress of a married man who was never going to leave his wealthy wife. So she went after me, although she had no intention of ever giving up her lover. Uncle Oliver thought I was just having some fun with her but when we announced our engagement—she threatened she'd leave me if I didn't marry her—he quickly revealed the ugly truth about her.'

Kitty's hand flew to her mouth. 'That's terrible. What a shock for you.'

'It wasn't a total shock. I was already having serious doubts about her, one reason being she became so critical of me. When I broke off with her she flew at me, screaming.' He shuddered. 'She was hateful and vindictive as she saw her meal ticket fly out the window. I had a very lucky escape.'

'Don't tell me—she made sure she got to keep the engagement ring.'

'I didn't care what she kept or how much it cost just so long as I didn't have to see her again. Needless to say, she was swiftly excluded from Uncle Olly's social circle. I felt like such a fool for having been taken in by her.'

'She sounds horrible,' Kitty said vehemently. 'And not very clever for treating a wonderful man like you in that way.'

'I'm glad you think I'm a wonderful man,' he said.

His words, the look in his eyes flustered her. 'Well, of course I do. Wonderful, yes. I... I wouldn't be working for you if I didn't think you were a wonderful man...person.'

'I happen to think you're a wonderful woman,' he said with his lazy grin.

'You do?'

'An exceedingly wonderful woman.'

'Are you teasing me?'

He sobered. 'Not at all. After my experience with Lavinia, I didn't let myself believe that wonderful women like you existed.'

'And now?'

'I'm here with you and feeling happier than I have for a long time.'

'Really?'

They were close in the confines of the car, with its polished walnut dash and leather upholstery that gave it a scent of luxury and wealth. He leaned over to kiss her, a warm tender kiss that said more than words could. She pressed her mouth to his to keep him there, not wanting the contact to end, barely able to believe this was happening.

'I'm happy to be with you too,' she murmured against his lips. She broke the kiss but stayed close, looking up into his eyes. 'The hospital car park is perhaps not the best place for this.'

'Perhaps not,' he said. 'But before I drive out of here I'd like you to tell me about that guy who doesn't deserve airtime.'

She sighed and drew back from him. 'I warn you, the story of me and Neil is nothing as interesting as you and Lavinia.'

'I'm not sure the drama of my story is anything to be proud of,' he said with a wry twist of his mouth.

'I met Neil at work when we both started at Blaine and Ball as interns. I don't remember ever consciously deciding I wanted a future with him; he just swept me along and we were having so much fun I let it happen.'

'Was it serious?'

'We lived together, had a future planned. I believed we were in love. It wasn't an angsty kind of relationship, if you know what I mean. We were a normal couple with our ups and downs, but nothing to indicate the way it would end.'

'I don't think I've ever had a non-angsty relationship, but I think I know what you mean.'

'Then came the assault.' She paused. Still the ugly memories came, Edmund Blaine's disgusting wet mouth on hers, his fingers that had hurt like claws, her feeling of powerlessness. 'I… I find this distressing to talk about, but I want you to hear, so bear with me.'

Sebastian took her hand, which comforted her. 'Take your time.'

'The night it happened, I staggered home in distress, expecting comfort, a hug. But he held me at arm's length because another man had touched me, as if I were tainted.'

Sebastian cursed in Spanish.

'That was the thing that brought my future with Neil unstuck—he believed me that I had been assaulted; however, no one else of any consequence in the company did. He wasn't going to be the lone dissenting voice—not when his career would suffer. When he made my pain all about him, that I selfishly wanted to ruin his career by forcing him to take sides, I told him to get out and he did. Essentially, he chose his job over me. End of story.' She had collapsed on the living room floor of their flat and cried until she had run out of tears.

Sebastian expressed his opinion of what kind of man Neil was in no uncertain terms.

'I was devastated at the time; we were on the point of getting engaged,' she said. 'On top of the assault, the nightmare media coverage, losing my job, the thought that someone I believed in—who was supposed to love me—could be so disloyal really...really wounded me. It left me with such trust issues I haven't dated since.'

He squeezed her hand. 'Last night?'

'The first time I've let anyone close since then.'

There was a long beat of silence between them before Sebastian leaned over to kiss her again. A swift touch that didn't demand or expect anything.

'He didn't deserve you,' he said gruffly.

'He most definitely did not. And for a long time I wondered what I'd done wrong to deserve him. But I got over missing him so quickly it made me wonder if I had ever really loved him enough to build a life with him. There had never been fireworks.' Not like the fireworks that had exploded when Sebastian had kissed her, not like that instant buzz of attraction when she'd first met him at his Docklands apartment.

'The breakup was why you had to use packers to get you quickly out of your home.'

'You remembered that?'

'I remember everything you've told me about you.'

'And...and me you.'

She didn't care that she was in a public car park, when Sebastian kissed her again nothing else mattered as she let herself enjoy the sensations of being close to him.

Finally, when the windows were beginning to fog up, she broke away from the second most wonderful kiss she had ever experienced, her body pulsing with desire. The first had been the night before. Whatever happened to them in the future, she would always cherish her first kiss with Sebastian, which had unleashed possibilities she had never allowed herself to dream of.

'What do we do now?' she asked, her breath still coming a little short, her heart beating in double time.

His voice wasn't steady. 'I know what I'd like us to do right now but, as you said, we're in a public car park.' He pressed a short fierce kiss on her mouth. 'However, I don't think that's what you meant. I suggest we keep our private lives private.'

'So things will be the same back in Chelsea? I would prefer that,' she said. 'In public, employee and boss—'

'Temporary boss,' he said.

'Temporary boss,' she amended. 'In private—'

'Whichever way we choose to take it,' he said.

'Whichever way we choose to take it…' she echoed.

They shared smiles for a long moment and Kitty felt something fundamental shift into place between them, on the edge of something that could be momentous and life-changing.

'Today at lunch can we be cautious? I'm still anxious about being seen—'

'Strictly business,' he said. He started the engine, coaxed it into a luxurious purr and put it into gear. 'To lunch, Ms Clements.'

'To lunch, Sir Sebastian,' she said.

They traded a warm, convivial laugh of shared secrets, possibilities and anticipation.

CHAPTER THIRTEEN

KITTY ENJOYED THE meetings she had with Sebastian and his executive assistant, Guy. Guy was older than both her and Sebastian, whip-smart, super organised, seemed to know everyone who was everyone, and had a marvellous ability to mimic them that often had her in stitches. He'd previously worked with Sebastian's uncle Oliver and had confessed to Kitty he'd had a huge crush on his boss that hadn't been in any way reciprocated. He'd been devastated when Oliver Delfont had died, and delighted when Sebastian had recently headhunted him from his last role to bring him back into the family.

Kitty tried to avoid any gossip about Sebastian, especially as she suspected eagle-eyed Guy would jump on any sign of her, Kitty, having a crush on her boss. Which she most definitely did. However, any crumb of information that would help her understand Sebastian better was welcome. According to Guy, Oliver Delfont had cared deeply for his nephew and had done his best to shield him from Sir Cyril's malice. Now Guy was committed to helping Sebastian shoulder the responsibilities of his new life as he had a wealth of useful knowledge from when he had worked with Oliver, anticipating the day he would have taken over from Sir Cyril.

On the Monday afternoon after the visit to Gramps, Kitty and Guy sat opposite Sebastian across his desk in his office. 'The dinner party for the trustees on Saturday was so successful I'm emboldened to think we should have a party to follow up. Perhaps in another two weeks. What do you think, Kitty?' He'd put forward this thought to her at their 'strictly business' lunch at the riverside pub the day before.

'If you think two weeks is notice enough for your guests,' she said.

Guy replied, 'I've put out a few feelers; it would work for most of the people we want here.'

'In that case, if we can get the same hospitality team together, I'm confident they will pull out all the stops for another successful party,' said Kitty. 'Although I'm not sure Evelyn Lim could perform the same miracle when it came to transforming rooms as quickly as she did for the dining room.'

'Even the small improvements she made to the reception rooms made a difference,' Sebastian said. 'If she could make a few more such changes, that would be good but not essential.'

'I'm speaking in confidence, as you know.' Se-

bastian leaned towards her and Guy as he spoke.
'Some of the trustees gave me disquieting news
about how the Lady Enid foundation was managed after she died. It was rumoured Sir Cyril
intended to dissolve it. Donations dropped off,
and confidence in the foundation's viability is at
an all-time low. I want to restore that confidence
and lift the level of donations.'

'A cocktail party for about fifty people,' said
Guy. 'Company directors, high-flying entrepre-
neurs, C-level executives—you know, where the
C stands for Chief in their work title.'

Fifty high-ranking business people, all involved
in some way or another with the Delfont enterprises and investments. Kitty quailed. That kind
of number upped the chance of someone recog-
nising her. All her old fears flooded back.

'Do you have the guest list handy?' she asked,
forcing her voice to sound even and professional.

Guy passed a sheet of paper to her. She quickly
scanned it. Yes. There were names she recognised
there, people who might in turn recognise her.
People she'd worked with on their PR campaigns
but who had cut her dead after she'd 'falsely accused a good man'.

'An impressive list,' she said.

She would make it clear to Sebastian from the
start she wouldn't be in attendance on the night.
Make a fuss about it now in front of Guy and he
might get suspicious of her motives. He knew she

was Kathryn Clements, there had been no point in hiding it from him, but he didn't know her whole story—nor did he need to.

She pasted a smile on her face. 'Do you want to set a theme for the party?'

'No.' The vehement answer from Sebastian was so definitive that it made Kitty and Guy laugh and she immediately felt less on edge.

Sebastian continued. 'I want the party to be relaxed and quite different from the stuffy parties I know my grandfather used to host.'

'To mark a change in direction from the new Delfont on the block,' Kitty said.

'Exactly,' he said.

'The cool new baronet on the block,' said Guy. 'Your uncle Oliver would be proud of the way you're handling this.'

'Uncle Olly certainly was one for a good party,' said Sebastian, but Kitty could see the remembered pain in the rigid set of his jaw.

She swung right back into event planner mode. 'So, a cocktail party on the agenda for the Saturday after next,' she said. 'I'm confident that our two cooks Alisa and Josie can create food that's fashionable yet delicious.'

'Can we have crostini on the menu?' Sebastian asked. Kitty's eyes met his across the desk.

'Of course,' she said with an inner secret smile, dropping her gaze in case she gave away the game to Guy. She didn't miss his speculative glance between her and Sebastian. They would have to be careful if they wanted to keep their changed relationship private. Until they knew where it might take them.

She continued, 'And we need to secure some really good bar staff specialising in cocktails—some call them mixologists. The drinks as well as the food need to be outstanding to get some buzz happening.'

Sebastian smiled. 'A party totally unlike anything my grandfather would have planned.'

'Indeed,' said Guy.

'One other thing we need to consider—music,' said Sebastian. 'Friends of mine from uni play in a soft jazz quartet. I'd like to book them.'

'Done,' said Guy. 'Just shoot me their details.'

How little she knew about Sebastian, Kitty thought, as he and Guy chatted. Yet what she did know about him pleased her very much. That chasm between them no longer seemed as deep as she might have imagined. Did she have the courage to take a leap over it?

Guy got up to go. Kitty did likewise.

'Kitty, can you stay behind, please,' Sebastian said. 'I'd like to talk about the food for the party in more detail.'

Guy left, closing the door behind him, making an elaborate show of closing it properly. *He knew.*

Sebastian immediately strode around the desk to Kitty.

'I'll talk to the cooks about the food and—' she started.

Sebastian made a dismissive gesture with his hand. 'I don't give a flying fig about the food.' He pulled her into his arms. 'During that entire meeting I just wanted to do this. I don't even remember what Guy said about the strategic importance of inviting two company directors with a known history of animosity towards my grandfather.'

Kitty looked up at him, his lean, handsome face already so familiar. 'Is it ridiculous to say I missed you, even though we've seen each other several times today?' she said. They'd talked, together with Evelyn Lim, about bathroom designs, bumped into each other as Kitty was leading housekeeper candidates into her office. But, until now, not for a second had they been alone.

'I've missed you too,' he said hoarsely.

The night before, after returning from Widefield, it had seemed an unspoken understanding that, while they'd kissed each other goodnight, they had each gone alone to their own rooms. It would have been too soon.

Kitty nestled in against his shoulder with a sigh of pleasure. For a long moment she was content to just be close to him in the circle of his arms. It was the first time they hadn't had coats as a barrier between them. Kitty was wearing her blue wrap dress, Sebastian black trousers and charcoal shirt. It would be so easy to unbutton his shirt and

slide her hand through to find warm, bare skin.
It seemed the natural next step, but surely it was
too soon for that. She was super aware of how
strong he was, the firmness of his muscles, the
solid comfort of him. Then that comforting closeness was no longer enough. With a murmur of
impatience she wound her arms around his neck,
pressed her body closer to his—close, closer, as
close as she could get with the pesky barrier of
their clothes. She couldn't wait any longer to feel
his mouth on hers and she reached up and kissed
him.

Their first kiss in private, behind a solid door
that no one would dare open without Sebastian's
say so. The kiss was immediate, urgent, snatched
from their everyday life in the house where she
was his household employee. It wasn't a kiss that
started with gentle questing lips and slowly built
up in increments of passion. It started hot and
proceeded to flaming in just seconds flat. Urgent.
Demanding. Greedy. Her nipples pebbled and she
was melting with want as she pressed her body
closer to him. She scoped out the room. There was
a desk, there was a leather Chesterfield sofa…
heck, there was the floor or the wall. Kitty whimpered her need for him and heard the same need
in his deep moan. She was lost in one of her own
fantasies of seducing her boss.

The tie of her wrap dress had loosened and he
slid his hand through where the top gaped open to

cup her breast and thumb her hard nipple so she gasped her pleasure and need.

Then a knock on the door. They stilled, then sprang apart. Sebastian cursed under his breath, as did Kitty. She rearranged her dress. The knock came again. Josie, today's cook, called through the door, 'Excuse me, Sir Sebastian, is Kitty still with you? I urgently need to talk to her about tonight's dinner menu.'

Kitty signalled with her eyes for his help. He cleared his throat. 'Yes, she's still in a meeting with me. I'll send her down to the kitchen when we're finished.' His voice sounded remarkably normal.

'Thank you,' Josie said, and Kitty listened until the cook's footsteps receded.

Kitty looked up at him, her lips curved in a teasing smile. 'Finish what, I might ask?' she murmured.

'Not what we were starting,' he said in his deep posh voice.

Kitty felt overwhelmed by the urge to laugh at the ridiculousness of it, a thirty-two-year-old baronet and owner of this grand house and her twenty-eight-year-old self compromised like a pair of hormone-crazed teenagers. She ached with the effort to suppress her giggles. What made it worse was that Sebastian was trying not to laugh too and they were setting each other off. They held each other as they both shook and spluttered until finally she was able to control her breathing and his voice returned to normal.

She stepped back from him, tugged her dress into place, pushed her hair back from her face where Sebastian had raked his fingers through it. She probably didn't have a scrap of lipstick left. 'Do you think Josie guessed?'

'I doubt it; we often have meetings in this room.' He paused. 'Perhaps it was fortuitous Josie came along when she did.' He drew her close to him. 'I don't want our first time to be rushed and uncomfortable.'

She followed his gaze to the wooden desk, the carved wooden chair. He smiled and she smiled back. Could he tell how thrilled she was at his words? *Our first time.* It sounded romantic, sexy and thoughtful—all of which augured well for, well, their first time.

He kissed her slowly and thoroughly. The fire of arousal that had been so abruptly doused by that knock on the door still smouldered, and little flames of desire started flickering through her. Reluctantly she pulled away.

'I don't think we'd get away with it a second time,' she said. 'I think Guy suspects something.'

'Perhaps,' said Sebastian. 'But he would be too discreet to gossip about it, I can assure you. He was loyal to my uncle and is loyal to me. I trust him as I've come to trust you.'

She kissed him briefly on the mouth. She, of

all people, knew how easily trust was lost and how hard it was to earn. 'I'm honoured,' she said.

She reached for her laptop case. In an inside pocket she kept a comb and a lipstick. Sebastian watched as she did a quick repair job. 'I've never seen a woman put on lipstick without a mirror,' he said.

'A trick I learned years ago from a friend.' She turned to go. 'I won't kiss you again as it would mess up my lipstick and I don't want to walk down to that kitchen looking like I've just been kissed.'

'Even though you have been kissed and you'll be thoroughly kissed again the second I get the opportunity.'

'I'll look forward to that,' she said. She trailed her fingers over his cheek in lieu of the kiss she ached to plant there, thrilling at the intimacy of the contact. But she didn't want people gossiping about her, especially in the run-up to the cocktail party.

She turned to go. Sebastian put his hand on her arm. 'Wait.' She turned back to face him.

'Dinner tonight?' he said.

'I'm not sure I—'

'Not at a restaurant. In the kitchen. Just you and me.'

There wouldn't be anyone else in the house. The cook would prepare the dinner and go home. Guy would go home to his husband.

'I'd love that,' she said.

* * *

That evening, Sebastian worked alongside Kitty in the kitchen as they heated up the chicken poached in coconut milk and Thai herbs Josie had prepared for dinner. The room was filled with warm spicy aromas that should send his mouth watering. But thoughts of Kitty overwhelmed every other sense. His hunger wasn't for the dinner, it was for her.

That blue dress, although it was long-sleeved and high-necked, did nothing to hide her luscious curves, or the way she moved with such grace and sensuality. All it did was emphasise how incredibly sexy she was and make him want to peel the dress off her to discover and explore those curves for himself.

Her grandfather Stan—in a moment when Kitty had been chatting with a nurse—had warned Sebastian not to let his granddaughter's prettiness and sweetness blind him into thinking she was anything less than very smart and very talented. Sebastian had known all that from the get-go— it was part of her appeal. Along the way, he'd learned that she was kind and funny and perceptive. It wasn't just her looks that attracted him, but right now they were top of mind. She was beautiful and alluring and all he could think about was how much he wanted her.

Kitty turned from the stovetop and caught him in full, heavy-lidded appraisal of her shapely behind. She knew immediately what he was doing and smiled a slow, lascivious smile as she let her eyes, in turn, roam over him. And succeeded in arousing him to fever pitch.

She put down the spoon she was holding. 'I don't think you're hungry at all.'

'Not for dinner, no, delicious as it undoubtedly would be,' he answered honestly.

'Me neither,' she said, switching off the gas burner and taking a step towards him. The invitation in her blue eyes was unmistakable and his body responded accordingly. 'This kitchen would be no more comfortable than your study,' she said.

'I imagine it would be exceedingly uncomfortable,' he said. 'Not to mention inappropriate for so many reasons.'

'A bed—vanilla as that might seem—comes to mind as the ideal place for our purposes,' she said in a silky, sensuous voice.

'It has a long-standing reputation as such,' he said, scarcely able to choke out the words.

'There is a very comfortable bed in my apartment, just a short elevator ride away,' she said.

He shuddered as politely as one could shudder. 'A room where Mrs Danvers once resided does not appeal.' An image of the bad-tempered old housekeeper flashing into his mind could put him off his stroke.

Kitty climbed her fingers up his arm. 'Can you nominate somewhere you believe to be more appropriate?'

'A beautifully appointed guest bedroom in this very house where I can personally attest to the comfort of the bed.'

'Shall we assess it for possibilities?' she murmured, sliding her arms around his neck and pressing her mouth to his. She flicked her tongue along the seam of his mouth. He moaned his want and opened his mouth to her. They kissed for a long, arousing moment before he disengaged from the kiss. He had to take a deep breath to steady his voice. 'Before we go any further, I have to ask you—are you sure this is what you want?'

Consent was essential from anyone, but particularly so from Kitty, who had suffered a heinous assault from someone she should have been able to trust. Kitty was important to him, and growing more important every day, until he was at the point where he couldn't imagine his life without her in it. He had to get this right.

'You absolutely have my consent, wonderful Sebastian.' To his stunned delight she then proceeded to whisper in his ear the intimate acts to which she was giving her wholehearted consent and how she would like to both receive and give them.

Sebastian growled his assent to anything she wanted, swung her up into his arms and headed for the stairs.

How many fantasies had Kitty had of making love with Sebastian since she'd come to live in his house? Even her most fervent and erotic dreams had nothing on the reality of being carried by Sebastian up the stairs and towards his bedroom. It was like a scene from one of his mother's books—only way sexier.

The journey from kitchen to Sebastian's bedroom was punctuated by laughter, kissing, stumbling as they tried to walk to the elevator while kissing, and a display of extreme impatience with the elevator. She felt giddy, not from the one glass of wine she'd had in the kitchen, but from desire, racing hormones and excitement. Over all the emotions she was feeling bubbled joy. She was falling for this man and enjoying every step of the journey. It was all so different and exciting because of him. Sebastian.

She didn't notice the details of the bedroom when they reached it, except that it was elegant in a Lady Enid style of way. But she didn't want to pause for breath to admire the room when all she wanted to do was to make love with Sebastian. Fortunately, he seemed as eager to make love with her.

They kissed, deeply, hungrily as if they could never get enough of each other. She unbuttoned his shirt to splay her hands against a hard wall of muscle. In her eagerness to undo the buttons one tore off and bounced to the floor. She gasped and went to pick it up. 'Leave it,' he said. She gladly complied. She didn't want to think about anything but him.

'How do you get this wrap thing undone?' Sebastian grumbled as he played with the ties that secured her dress at the waist.

'How about I stand still and let you undress me,' she said, loving the look of eager impatience on his face.

'Great idea,' he said hoarsely.

It felt intensely erotic to put herself into his hands and stand still as he undid the ties of her dress, as he pushed it off her shoulders, as he touched her anywhere he felt so inclined. Every such touch sent urgent messages through her body to all those erogenous zones he'd unlocked simply by being him.

Her dress pooled on the floor and she stepped out of it to stand just in her underwear and high-heeled shoes.

'Wow,' he breathed. He stood back and looked over her, every glance a caress as real as if he were actually touching her. 'You have the most beautiful body,' he said.

Kitty had to swallow the response that had been automatic until she'd fought to suppress it. *I just need to lose a few pounds*. He thought she was beautiful just the way she was and she should accept that unconditionally. 'Thank you,' she said instead.

'Now you,' she ordered. She started to undo the

rest of the buttons on his shirt, button by button, but her fingers fumbled in her haste. 'Darn it, I just want this shirt off you.' She struggled with his belt. 'And your trousers.'

He laughed, shrugged off his shirt, kicked off his shoes and stepped out of his trousers, leaving him in only black boxers that made no secret of how ready he was for her.

'Oh, my,' she sighed at the sight of his broad shoulders, powerful chest and six-pack belly. 'When it comes to beautiful bodies...' She took a deep breath. 'I just want to kiss you all over.'

'Please don't hesitate to start,' he said, flinging his arms wide in invitation.

As she kissed first his mouth then down his jawline, tasting him, stroking him with her tongue, down the strong column of his throat, across his shoulders, he was caressing her breasts, removing her bra, sliding his hand down her waist to cup her bottom and caress inside her panties.

She looked up at him, whimpered. 'Enough of the slow burn. I can't wait any longer. Please.' They were on the bed in seconds, with all remaining underwear discarded and tossed aside.

She stilled. 'Protection. I didn't think...'

'I did,' he said, reaching for the bedside drawer. No fantasy could match the sensation as he pushed inside her, filling her, thrilling her, taking her rapidly to orgasm. But it was more than sexual pleasure—it was a sensation on a different level that urged her to believe they were meant to be lovers.

Their first time was urgent, hungry and utterly perfect. Their second time was slow and thorough as they explored each other's bodies. It was also utterly perfect. To Kitty it seemed as if they had been waiting for each other, and that everything in her life had built up to this moment. Him. Sebastian. The man she had fallen in love with without really realising it had happened. She should be panicking because she had only known him for less than a month, but at a deep soul level she believed he felt the same way.

She woke very early the next morning to find herself lying with his arm slung possessively over her chest. He looked so beautiful when he was asleep. His black hair was ruffled from when she'd run her fingers through it, his face relaxed, dark stubble shadowing his jaw. The linen sheet was rucked up around his hips and she took a long moment to admire his body, his smooth olive skin, his muscled chest with just the right amount of dark hair, his powerful shoulders. She shivered with remembered pleasure of their lovemaking and felt boneless with desire.

Regretfully, she went to slide out of the bed so as not to awaken him. She had to get up and back to the apartment on the next floor before anyone arrived at the house: the daily cleaners she had engaged, Alisa the cook whose day it was on the job share, Guy, Evelyn's team of builders and decorators.

But a strong arm shot out and clamped her to the bed. 'Don't go,' Sebastian commanded. Remarkably, she didn't feel self-conscious or uncomfortable at finding herself naked in Sir Sebastian's bed. The easy repartee they'd established had translated well into lovemaking. They had quickly discovered each other's needs with anticipation of more to be learned.

'I thought you were asleep,' she murmured. 'I have to go, so no one sees me leaving your bedroom to take the walk of shame up to my apartment.'

'Why can't you stay? There's absolutely nothing to be ashamed of.' He pushed himself up on one elbow. The sheet slid away to reveal the full glory of his body. 'This is my house. We're both single, not hurting anyone by being together. I'm not really your boss, you're a contractor so we're not bending any employment laws.'

Kitty screwed up her face. 'I'd just be happy to not have the change in our relationship subject to scrutiny. Not…not just yet.'

She wanted to hug to themselves this wondrous thing that had flowered between them. Gossip and innuendo, the revival of her scandalous past, would only sully something that was beautiful and new and so very special. She tried to explain that to him.

'I understand,' he said. 'For now.'

'Thank you,' she said. 'I'm not ashamed, just cautious.' She kissed him.

'Are you sure you want to leave?' He slid a hand down her shoulder and cupped her breast.

'I find it impossible to resist you, Sir Sebastian,' she said, falling back into his arms until they were skin to skin.

CHAPTER FOURTEEN

NINE DAYS LATER, on the Thursday before the party, Sebastian was getting fed up with skulking around with Kitty in his own home. She spent each night in his bed. There were snatched kisses and surreptitious hugs whenever they had a private moment during the day. They went for long evening walks holding hands, along the Thames and around Chelsea, wearing hats and scarves up around their faces so they couldn't be recognised. But in front of anyone else it was no touching, no kissing and business as usual.

It wasn't enough. He wanted more, so much more. When he'd woken up the morning after the night they'd first made love and seen Kitty's blonde head next to him on the pillow, he'd known he was in love with her. In the past, he'd questioned if he had ever truly been in love. Now he knew he hadn't. He had never felt this depth of emotion for a woman before and he fell more in love with her every day. So much for Lavinia's cruel words: he *was* able to love. He'd loved his parents and his uncle. He loved his Spanish *abuela*. He just hadn't loved Lavinia.

Although no one had exactly come out and said they knew about the change in his relationship with Kitty, Sebastian suspected the people working in the house were aware. Guy almost certainly knew, but he was too much the professional to say anything. The cooks had guessed; it wouldn't have been difficult for them to know he and Kitty ate dinner together. He suspected Evelyn Lim knew too. But he got the distinct feeling they were all happy for him and Kitty, and okay with pretending they didn't know if that was what was required of them. Claudia knew—apparently she'd guessed Kitty's secret the second she'd seen Kitty the day after they'd first made love.

Sebastian wanted to tell her grandfather, Stan, that he and Kitty were a couple. He wanted to tell his *abuela* he had a lovely English girlfriend, as she worried that he wasn't married at thirty-two. He wanted to go public with the woman he loved. Not that he'd told her he loved her. It seemed too soon to actually put it into words.

When Kitty next popped into his office with a query about the arrangements for Saturday's party, he shut the door, took her in his arms for a swift hug and faced her. 'I want to talk to you about something really important to me.'

'Fire away,' she said.

'I want you to act as hostess at the party on Saturday. I know you said you wouldn't do it again—'

'Under any circumstances, if I recall my words correctly,' she said.

'But this would be very different to the last time. I don't want to fib about us being "just friends" when you mean so much more to me than that. I want you by my side as my girlfriend.'

She smiled. 'So I'm your official girlfriend now.'

'Something like that. If you prefer not to put a label on what we have together, I'm okay. My woman, perhaps, although that does sound rather beating-on-the-chest caveman stuff.'

'I'm fine with girlfriend. However, *boyfriend* doesn't seem dignified enough for you. But I can't really call you my lover; it seems way too intimate.'

'Probably not,' he said. 'Though feel free to say it in private.'

'Partner?' she said.

'Seems like a business partner. You already have one of those.'

'Gentleman friend?'

'A hundred years out of date, perhaps?'

'My guy?'

'Too casual.'

'Okay. Boyfriend it is. I'll try to think of something better. In the meantime, maybe I'll call you Sir Boyfriend.'

He groaned. 'Please, no. But does that mean you'll come to the party?'

'There will be people there who knew me in another life, who believed I—'

'Do you honestly think that people who owe a substantial part of their livelihood to the Delfont dominated companies would dare to criticise my girlfriend?'

'Perhaps not,' she conceded.

'I'm not like your jerk of an ex, Neil.'

'You're certainly not like him in any way.'

'I'm one hundred per cent on your side. I know how fiercely independent you are, and how you'll tell me you don't want my protection, but I want you to know you've got it.'

'Whether I like it or not?' she said.

'I wouldn't put it quite like that,' he said.

'Yes, you would,' she said with a smile. 'And I'll surprise you by saying I will accept your protection.'

'Seriously?' he said. 'Why the change of mind?'

'Something Gramps said about looking after each other.'

'He's a wise man, your grandfather.'

'He is, and I haven't always listened to him.' She paused. 'There's something else. Something that might tip me back into the media glare I hate so much, no matter how I try to hide from it.'

He frowned. 'What could that be?'

'Can we sit down?' she said.

He led her to the chesterfield sofa that Uncle Olly used to have in his study. He and Kitty had taken to sitting next to each other, rather than across the desk.

He took her hand in his. 'I'm intrigued.'

'Do you remember me telling you about my direct manager at Blaine and Ball, a woman named Hilary?'

'The one who told you to grin and bear it when the director started acting out of line?'

'That's the one. She contacted me yesterday and we met this morning for coffee on the King's Road.'

'Why did she want to see you? To apologise?'

'Oddly enough, yes. She confessed that she too was a victim of Edmund Blaine, and that there had been others.'

'What? And she did nothing to protect you?'

'Difficult to understand, isn't it? But she told me she was a single mum and he held the threat of losing her job over her.'

Sebastian frowned. 'I still don't like what she let happen to you when she could have protected you. Surely that makes her complicit.'

'I have mixed feelings about that too. I could barely look her in the eye, to tell you the truth. But what she said proved what I'd always suspected: that I couldn't have been the first and wouldn't be the last. What Hilary wanted to talk to me about was his latest victim. Edmund didn't realise when he tried to assault a pretty young intern that she was a martial arts expert and fought back. Not only that, she recorded the incident on her phone, then went home and showed it to her lawyer father.'

'In other words, he's in trouble.'

'Not necessarily. His defence is that it was a one-off incident brought on by stress. Hilary wants his other victims to come forward to say "me too", and establish a pattern of similar previous assaults.'

'Including you.'

'Including me, yes.'

'Will you do it?' he said.

'If others come forward, I will too. It's the only chance I have to fight back and clear my name.'

'Are you sure you want to put yourself through all that again?'

'I don't want to, of course not. But if it means that horrible man gets what he deserves it will be worth it. It could be my only chance to restore my reputation.'

Sebastian felt a fierce urge to protect Kitty. He held her close. 'Whatever happens, I'm there for you.'

'Thank you. And I want to be there for you. I'll come to the party, as your girlfriend.' Her voice softened. 'I'll be proud to.'

* * *

Kitty headed back to her office. In truth, the party was shaping up to be so good she had found herself wishing she could be there to enjoy it, instead of sitting the evening out in the kitchen.

But was it a step too far to use the event as the official 'outing' of her as Sebastian's girlfriend? She had to take the plunge some time. It was getting harder to hide the fact they were a couple, to keep it secret from everyone but Claudia. There was also the fact she didn't want to hide it any more; she wanted to be with him all the time. She had never felt happier with a man—although she was still intent on protecting her heart. It was early days yet—fireworks and flames could fizzle out as quickly as they flared.

But she wanted the freedom to pursue her relationship with him out in the open. Sebastian was giving her that opportunity by asking her to be by his side at the party. He masked it well, but she knew he was shy and must be secretly dreading meeting all those people. She knew she could help ease the way by being there. He wouldn't say it because he wouldn't want to pressure her, but he needed her.

She still dreaded the idea of encountering people who believed she had attempted to seduce an older married man and then when he'd refused her advances had reported him for assault as payback.

But now there was a very good chance that man would soon be exposed for the monster he was. Surely that would generate better headlines than raking up her old so-called scandal.

CHAPTER FIFTEEN

SEBASTIAN'S HOUSE WAS filled with music, the rise and fall chatter of people having a good time and the occasional burst of laughter. In other words, Kitty thought—not without a sense of pride—all the signs of a successful party in full swing.

While she was a guest—being Sebastian's girlfriend had elevated her status—she was also the event planner who had worked hard to get all this running so smoothly. In a moment she'd pop down to the kitchen, just to check there would be no interruptions to the so far seamless flow of silver trays filled with delicious cocktail snacks circulating around the guests, borne by charming 'resting' actors who moonlighted as waiters between gigs.

She and Sebastian had started the evening standing resolutely side by side to greet the guests. He'd introduced her as Kitty Clements, after all they were dating now, and she couldn't hide behind Kitty Rose. As he'd predicted, no one looked at her askance or said anything untoward and she'd begun to relax. The dinner party had passed without incident; why shouldn't the party be the same?

She was glad she'd invested in a credit-card-bruising new dress for the occasion—a flattering aqua silk sheath overlaid with a silver-threaded lace that gave a subtle touch of bling. It had a modest vee neckline, elbow-length sleeves and came to just a few inches above her knees.

That afternoon, she'd visited the hairdresser to have her hair done up in a messy bun, and she wore her favourite turquoise and silver earrings. She'd had a manicure and taken extra care with her make-up. All in all, she was confident she looked less housekeeper and more Cinderella as Sir Sebastian's date for the evening. Sebastian looked devastatingly handsome in a dark suit. But then Sebastian looked devastatingly handsome in anything he wore, and even more handsome in nothing at all, as she'd been recently privileged to discover.

But while she and Sebastian had chatted with guests—the renovation of Sir Cyril's house was a popular topic—they'd somehow spun away from each other. He was now several groups of people away from her and, at the realisation, Kitty felt a flutter of panic. She couldn't do this on her own. He was her anchor in a sea of unknown faces. She managed to catch his eye and indicated she was going to head down to the kitchen. He nodded and gave her his special smile that reassured her, even across the room, he had her back. If her heart showed in her eyes when she smiled back at him, she didn't care. There was a gratifying freedom in not having to pretend otherwise.

She left the room and headed down the short corridor that led to the kitchen stairs, her thoughts turning to the food. Several people had asked her for the name of the excellent caterers, and she'd been happy to tell them it was Sebastian's own staff. She wanted to tell Alisa and Josie; they'd be pleased at the compliment.

Someone grabbed her roughly by the top of her arm and spun her around to face them. 'Hey! Let go of—' she started, but the words stopped on her tongue. Edmund Blaine glared down at her, face red, eyes bulging, his alcohol-tinged breath nauseating her. Like a nightmare come to life. His grip on her left arm was so hard it hurt. All the remembered terror of the night he'd assaulted her rushed back like a black fog smothering her brain. She froze, as if her feet were glued to the floor.

'Well, well, look who's weaselled her way into somewhere she doesn't belong,' he sneered.

But she did belong here. His words pierced her terror, deflating it. She was a different person from that girl he'd assaulted, and no longer his victim. Using moves she'd learned in her self-defence classes, she chopped at his hand that gripped her arm and kicked hard at his kneecap with her silver stiletto shoe. Taken by surprise, he stumbled back from her, uttering a string of foul expletives.

'You're the one who doesn't belong here. Your name isn't on the guest list.' She could not let him know she was shaking inside.

'I was close to Sir Cyril. On the boards of his companies.'

His hateful name on the guest list would have shone out as if neon lit. Had it been added later? She could not, would not, believe Sebastian had knowingly invited this man to his home.

'This is Sir Sebastian's party.'

'Your *boyfriend.*' The way he sneered the word made it sound like something dirty. 'Wouldn't he like to know the truth about you.'

'He knows the truth about *you*,' Kitty retorted before she realised it was pointless engaging in any kind of conversation with this loathsome man.

'He'll believe my version of what happened over yours,' he said. 'Then we'll see who'll flounce around boasting about her rich boyfriend. Watch for the headlines when I leak an update on what I discovered about you tonight to my favourite news editor.'

Kitty clenched her teeth. Nausea and fury roiled inside her. She could not show her fear and revulsion—this man thrived on it. Nor could she tell him he'd be getting his comeuppance very soon when the women he'd hurt spoke out against him.

They were keeping that confidential until their numbers were finalised.

'Get out,' she said.

'Yeah. I'll find your boyfriend and let him know exactly what kind of little hussy he's got himself mixed up with.'

He limped away—quite a bad limp, Kitty was pleased to note. If she'd broken his kneecap, she'd be glad.

An elegantly dressed woman—not his wife—rushed to him, giving Kitty a haughty, disapproving stare. It was meant to put her in her place, the 'hired help' place, and Kitty cringed from it. She'd told Edmund she belonged here, but did she?

She wanted to push past Edmund and find Sebastian before he did, but she knew her shaky legs wouldn't carry her that far and she was in danger of collapse. She staggered to the guest bathroom and locked the door. As the room spun, she fought the nausea but she feared she was about to faint. She sank down onto the chair, braced her head between her hands and lowered it to her knees. Gradually she started to feel better, and she slowly got up from the chair. Steadier now on her feet, she took a few deep breaths then splashed cold water on her face. She fixed the resulting mascara run with a tissue and took more deep breaths to compose herself.

By the time she got back to the party, Sebastian should have shown Edmund the door. But, to her shock, Edmund was still there, in the middle of the room and engaged in conversation with Sebastian. Was her boyfriend booting the older man out? It didn't appear so. In fact their conversation appeared to be downright convivial.

Kitty couldn't believe it when she saw Sebastian lay a hand on Edmund's arm. Then he laughed—Sebastian actually laughed at something Edmund had said. Edmund had told her Sebastian would believe his version of what had gone down between the two of them years ago. Were they laughing at her? And what was Edmund doing here in the first place? No way would she have agreed to be at this party if she'd had any inkling he'd be here too. By schmoozing with Edmund—knowing full well what he'd done to her—Sebastian was as bad as Neil. He was so engrossed in the discussion that he didn't see her. But Edmund did, and shot her a look of malevolent triumph.

Kitty felt her heart shrivel up until it was a dried-out husk. Again that social chasm loomed between her and Sir Sebastian. How could she have optimistically imagined it could be ignored? As she stood watching her lover in conversation with her abuser, it seemed as if the priceless Persian carpet on the floor between them tore in half and the floorboards cracked and opened up a dark black sink hole that ran beneath London—particularly this part of London.

Edmund came from the same kind of family

as Sebastian had—not the Spanish side, but the Delfont side—public school, Oxbridge, gentlemen's clubs, the arrogant privileges one could only be born into. That upper echelon that she had joked went way beyond the A-list. So very different from her background. How could she imagine that anything more could develop between her and Sebastian?

He cared for her, she was sure he did, although he had never actually said he loved her. And she loved him. But there could be no tomorrow for them. Sebastian would probably reach that way of thinking himself, perhaps when it was time to produce an heir. But it was Kitty who would end it— right now. Because she could not live with a man who was talking and laughing so jovially with the person who had caused her so much trauma. A man who knew how that encounter and the betrayals that followed had wounded her. It was a searing pain that cut right through her and she couldn't imagine she would ever recover from it.

No guest rushed to talk to her, standing there alone on the fringe of other people's conversations. All her old insecurities came rushing back. She was worthy of attention from these people only when she was part of the Sebastian/Kitty act—not for herself. Perhaps she hadn't played her role well enough. She was the downstairs girl allowed upstairs to join in the party, the downstairs girl who had had the temerity to move upstairs to the master's bed.

She had to leave this house. Now. For good. She had one more week on the contract, but she couldn't endure being here for a moment longer.

Kitty straightened her back, pasted a socially acceptable smile on her face, turned her back on the unbearable sight of the man she had grown to love in conversation with the man who had assaulted her then blackened her name and ended her career, and headed towards the elevator that would take her up to the housekeeper's apartment.

Sebastian had just delivered the news to Edmund Blaine that he was fired from his directorships of the Delfont companies, and that if he didn't leave the house this second he would call his security guards and have him charged with trespassing, when he looked over to see Kitty heading away from the main throng of party guests. Her back was unnaturally rigid, her footsteps too carefully placed, as if she feared falling. *Why?*

With a firm grip on the older man's elbow, he steered Blaine to the door and told him in a threatening undertone exactly what he could expect if he had anything to do with him or his girlfriend again. And that he would sue him to kingdom come if any damaging stories about Kitty appeared in any media, conventional or online. If he could have booted Blaine in the rear end to send him tumbling head over heels down the marble stairs he would have done so, but that would have placed him in the wrong. And the man was not worth being charged with assault.

Now he needed to find Kitty. There was something about the way she'd held herself that had worried him. As he headed towards where he had last seen her, one of his guests caught his arm and it was all he could do not to shake her off. By the time he'd exchanged pleasantries, Kitty was gone.

He didn't want to make it obvious he was looking for her; she would hate having attention drawn to her. But a subtle search showed she wasn't with any of the guests in the party area or the kitchen. Guy, walking by with two colourful cocktails in hand, told him he'd seen Kitty on her way to the elevator.

To touch up her make-up and do girly things? That couldn't be right. Eminently practical Kitty could do those things without the aid of a mirror. Sebastian headed for the elevator.

There was no light coming from under the door to the housekeeper's flat. He knocked on the door. No answer. He knocked again. 'Kitty,' he called softly. His voice hung still in the hallway. He tried the handle of the door, was surprised when it opened under his hand. 'Are you okay?' he called. But his words echoed back at him. As he pushed the door open, he was overwhelmed by a sense of foreboding.

Kitty was gone.

There was a coldness to the rooms that had nothing to do with the time of year and everything to do with her absence. Empty clothes hangers hung in the wardrobe. The bathroom shelf was bare, and nothing out of place in the kitchenette. His grey cashmere scarf lay folded neatly on an arm of the sofa—a gift resoundingly rejected. The rooms were empty, yet her floral fragrance lingered on the air, taunting him. He felt as if he'd been hurtled into some alternate reality where everything had turned upside down.

Where was she?

Something shiny glinted from under the sofa and he bent to retrieve it. One glittering silver high-heeled shoe, discarded after the party, missed in what must have been a hasty packing. He looked at the shoe for a long time.

Kitty had been so bright and vivacious at the party in her shimmering dress, these sexy shoes and her knockout smile. She'd known exactly what to say to make him look good and endear herself to some of the crustiest of characters. She'd charmed several on-the-spot promises of donations to the foundation out of the most unlikely of people. He was so proud of her. What the hell had happened?

Then he saw the note. A page torn from a note-book, propped up against the bookshelf, the words hastily scrawled. His hand shook as he picked it up, dreading what he might read.

Sebastian,
I can't do this. It's not going to work for us and I can't face living here. How could you have welcomed the man who attacked me into this house, a place where I felt so safe?
Please consider this the termination of my contract. I'm sorry if I've let you down, but the staff I've put in place all know what they're doing. You don't need me.
Kitty

The words hit him like a punch to the gut. *You don't need me.*

How wrong could she be? A rush of anguish swept over him, so powerful he had to hold onto the back of the sofa. He needed her more than he'd ever needed anyone. He needed her, wanted her, *loved* her. Regret smote him like a sledgehammer. *Yet he hadn't told her he loved her.*

Her leaving shouldn't surprise him. This party had been a huge deal for her. Not just the organising of it, but accompanying him as his girlfriend. She must have faced down the same fear and trepidations she had for the foundation dinner party— worse, as she'd known there could be people here who knew her. He should never have strayed from her side. Her worst nightmare come true would have been the presence of Edmund Blaine.

She obviously hadn't seen him kick the odious guy out of the house. He had to find her, had to explain.

But he still had a houseful of guests downstairs. If he disappeared now it would cause a ripple of gossip that would widen to include Kitty. He knew she would hate that. And it would negate all the good work she had done here.

Where would she have gone? To Claudia? Sebastian realised he didn't know where Kitty's friend and business partner lived. Or would she have gone home to her grandfather's house? That was more likely.

He would go back to the party now, then in the morning find out where Kitty had gone, tell her all the things he should have told her before this—and hope she would forgive him. He wanted a second chance with Kitty.

Kitty got out of the cab at Victoria Station. It wasn't yet nine p.m. There were still trains for Widefield to take her to the security of home. As she wheeled her two small suitcases to the platform, the enormity of what she had done hit her. She started to shake, had to stop and pull her coat around her.

She'd left Sebastian without saying goodbye. Sneaked quietly out of the house while the party went on around her. Had he noticed she'd gone? This morning she'd woken up entwined in his arms, feeling happy and safe and, yes, in love. Safe no longer. In love no longer. The flames of her shock and anger at the sight of him being so chummy with Edmund Blaine still smouldered. She could think of no worse betrayal on Sebastian's part than welcoming that heinous man into his house. It was as if he had rejected her and all they'd shared.

CHAPTER SIXTEEN

SEBASTIAN HAD BARELY slept for thinking about Kitty and how badly things had gone wrong. He'd beaten himself up for the whole stupid idea of employing her instead of following his instinct and being honest with both her and himself about his attraction to her. Instead of telling her exactly how he felt.

But now he faced the morning with determination. He would fix this. He would win her back. He would do whatever he had to do. Even if he had to grovel. But to do so, he might need an ally. And he knew just the person to enlist.

He was up early enough to book a suite for himself at a luxury boutique hotel not far from Widefield and be on the road to Kent. He would not return to Cheyne Walk without fighting for a second chance with Kitty.

He was convinced Kitty would have gone to her grandfather's house, not least because she had told him before the party that she would be heading down to the rehab hospital the next morning. He had offered to drive her; she had accepted. Now he could only assume she would visit her grandfather under her own steam. He'd been looking forward to seeing Stan again; he'd liked the older man a lot. Now he might have to enlist his help.

Kitty woke up in the bedroom that had been hers since she was fourteen years old. A feeble sun was filtering through the daisy-patterned curtains she'd never let Gran update; they represented continuity and security to her. She'd always thought of this house as her haven. Now, for the first time, she didn't feel at home here. And she felt so very alone without Sebastian by her side.

What had she done?

The right thing. She reminded herself of the terror and loathing that had overwhelmed her when Edmund Blaine had grabbed her, and then again at his look of malicious gloating over Sebastian's shoulder when he'd noticed her staring at them.

He'll believe my version of what happened over yours, he'd boasted.

Was that why Sebastian had been so convivial with her attacker? Had he believed him? In her heart of hearts, Kitty couldn't believe that. And yet he had had his hand on Edmund's arm like an old friend.

Had Sebastian perhaps not realised to whom he was speaking in such a friendly manner? Not possible. Edmund would have made it very clear who he was before he'd starting spilling poison about her.

The fact was, Edmund came from Sebastian's world and she didn't. She'd been foolish to imagine she could fit in.

But she didn't feel as though she fitted in this world any more either.

The night before, when she'd arrived by train at Widefield, she'd started off on the well-lit and well-trod way to Gramps's house, only to be stopped by her high school boyfriend, Owen, who'd just dropped a friend at the station for the London train. Owen, as good-looking and nice as ever, had insisted on driving her home and checking all was okay at the house. She'd been in no mood for chatting, but had forced herself to be polite. He'd suggested they meet up for a drink. For a moment she'd been tempted. He was smart and funny and single and felt utterly familiar.

But he wasn't Sebastian.

And she didn't want to be with any other man but him. *Ever.*

She forced herself up and out of bed. The bathroom wasn't quite finished but she could have a shower and get ready to go visit Gramps. She'd probably burst into tears at his first kind word, but she knew he would always be on her side.

An hour and a half later, Kitty wasn't so sure about that. She'd arrived at the rehab hospital to visit Gramps, only to be stopped in her tracks at the sight of her grandfather deep in conversation with Sebastian. She gasped, speechless, as she was swept by a feeling of déjà vu—Sebastian in the small chair next to Gramps in the larger one, his leg in a surgical boot, his crutches nearby.

'Kitty.' Gramps smiled at her, sheepishly she thought.

Sebastian immediately rose from his chair to greet her. She was wearing flat boots, jeans, a plain white shirt and a navy-blue hooded parka she'd had since high school, and felt at a distinct disadvantage. In his black jeans and superbly cut charcoal jacket he looked just like a baronet visiting someone else's grandfather should look. But his eyes were shadowed and wary.

'Kitty,' he said, his gaze never leaving her face. 'You had me worried. Are you okay?'

'Perfectly fine,' she said stiffly. 'I caught the train home.'

'I was looking forward to seeing Stan so I—'

'Came on your own,' she said tartly, glaring at him.

'Yes,' he said.

Gramps looked from Kitty to Sebastian and back again. 'I can see you're not happy, love, but there are always two sides to every story. Sebastian has told me his side of what happened last night. I know he wants to tell it to you.' She went to protest but Gramps put up his hand. 'I think you'll want to hear it.'

'I feel I've been hijacked,' she said, swallowing a sob. How could Gramps do this to her?

'Blame me for that,' Sebastian said gruffly. 'This was the only way I thought I could get you to see me. I've been calling you all morning.'

'I've had my phone switched off,' she said in a tone as offhand as she could make it.

'Come on, love,' said Gramps. 'You don't want to be the entertainment here for the other old folks.'

'I'll go,' said Sebastian. He turned away from her, but not before she'd seen his expression of utter devastation.

'No. Wait. I… I'll hear you out. But not here.' Gramps was right; eyes were turning in their direction.

'Don't worry about me,' said Gramps. 'I've got a card game going with a few mates I've made here.'

She had to do this. Let Sebastian know how much he'd wounded her. It wouldn't make any difference to her decision to go. But at least she'd get the chance to say goodbye.

She followed Sebastian out to where his car was parked. 'I don't want to talk in your car,' she said, remembering the passionate kisses she had shared with him the last time she'd been here.

'I'm booked into a hotel not far from here.' The

only hotel nearby was a very swish boutique hotel in a converted Georgian mansion. 'We could go there to talk if that suits.'

They were speaking to each other like strangers. Not lovers who had joyously explored each other's bodies. It was heartbreaking.

He got out his car keys.

'No,' she said. 'Er, not *no* to the hotel but no to going in your car. I'll follow you in mine.' No way would she let herself get trapped.

He shrugged. 'If that's what you want, Kitty.'

Of course it wasn't what she wanted. She wanted to be laughing with him with the old ease they'd felt from the get-go, to be swept into his arms and hugged close.

This was a nightmare.

'It's what I want,' she said, clamping down on any hint of her tumultuous emotions creeping into her voice.

In her somewhat battered small hatchback, she drove behind him for the ten minutes it took to reach the circular gravel drive of the hotel, swallowing hard against the persistent sob that seemed determined to break out, blinking away tears she refused to let him see.

She parked the car next to his, thinking bleakly that the difference in their situations was blatant even in the cars they drove.

Inside, the hotel was exquisitely decorated in a subdued elegance with a nod to the building's history and a deference to modern expectations of comfort. But she barely noticed it.

'I'll order lunch to be sent up to my suite,' he said.

She'd been alone with him so many times, why did this feel so awkward?

'I couldn't eat a thing,' she muttered.

In the elevator she stood as far away as she could in silence. And then they were in his suite, a stylish living area with two fat, overstuffed sofas placed opposite each other, the bedroom dominated by a modern version of a four-poster bed. She refused to let her eyes be drawn to the bed.

Sebastian had never seen Kitty look so uncomfortable. She stood apart from him as if dreading any inadvertent touch. Her face was drawn and wan as if all the light had gone out of her. Had he extinguished that sunshine that had always spilled onto him?

'Why did you leave Cheyne Walk?'

Why did you leave me?

'Didn't you read my note?' Her voice was laced with sadness so profound his heart clenched.

'I did and it puzzled me. I thought things were working out well for us. You were brilliant last night. I was so proud of you. So happy you were by my side.'

'So why were you schmoozing with Edmund Blaine? What was he doing there in the first place?' Her blue eyes were dark with accusation and pain. He hated to see her like that. He wanted to take her in his arms and comfort her, but she'd thrown up a barrier around herself, invisible but impenetrable.

'Schmoozing? You seriously think I was *schmoozing* with that man?'

'That's what it looked like. What was he doing there? Of all places, I thought I was safe from him in your house. Yet when I left to check on things in the kitchen, he came up behind me, accosted me, threatened me, *frightened* me, told me he was going to spin more lies about me, this time to you. Did you notice he was limping? That was because of me. I had to kick him in the knee to stop him from touching me.'

'Kitty. No. I'm so sorry.' He should have thrown that monster down the stairs.

'I came to warn you about him but he beat me to it. And I saw you chatting with him as if he were an honoured guest, laughing, even putting your hand on his arm.' Her face crumpled and she shuddered in revulsion. 'How could you? When you knew his history with me?'

'I'm horrified you should think that. You have to believe me. My encounter with Blaine wasn't like that at all.'

'It wasn't?' Her eyes narrowed suspiciously.

'For one thing, he wasn't an honoured guest. He was a gate-crasher.'

'What do you mean?'

'Odd to apply that term to a middle-aged man, but there it is. He was limping when he approached me, so it must have been just after his encounter with you. I couldn't put a name to most of the guests, as you know, and had no idea who he was. He wanted to reminisce about Sir Cyril, of whom he was a great admirer. Needless to say, that didn't go down well with me. I was about to make my excuses and circulate when he introduced himself. I recognised the name straight away. He must have seen something in my face as he made a joke of not having received an invitation, told me it must have been an oversight on my part.'

'He really had the gall to come to your party uninvited?'

'As if it were his due. I didn't say anything. I could tell he thought he had me fooled.'

'Had totally underestimated you, you mean.' At last a warming of the coldness in her eyes.

'I played him like I'd seen Sir Cyril play a trout at the end of his line when he'd dragged me and my father in our time of exile up to a cousin's Scottish estate.'

'Tell me,' she said.

'He reminded me he sat on the boards of two Delfont companies—both of which I knew were particularly well remunerated—in a public relations advisory capacity. There was a lot of blah-

blah-blah about how Sir Cyril had valued him. And the underlying, terribly polite insinuation I could never be the man my grandfather was. He's like one of the loathsome boys who bullied me so mercilessly at that private school when I was nine.'

'Yet he can be charming,' she said.

'As the worst bullies can be,' he said. 'That's when I started looking around for you, then remembered you'd gone down to the kitchen.'

'Me? Surely you couldn't believe I wanted to meet him?'

'Of course not. But I thought you might enjoy being with me when I fired him from his directorships.'

'You fired him? But you were being so chummy with him. You even had your hand on his arm, like you were best buddies.'

'I wasn't being chummy. What you must have seen was me laughing at his preposterous suggestion he was the innocent party in the scandal two years ago. The hand on his arm was me restraining him and telling him, with a pleasant expression on my face so I didn't alert the party guests to what was happening, that if he didn't leave right then I'd call our security guards and have him arrested for trespassing.'

'But you don't have security guards.'

'He didn't know that. But even then he continued to slander you. So I fired him, told him what I would do to him if he did or said anything that could harm you, and personally escorted him from the house.'

'You did? But I didn't see…' She paused. 'Because I was so upset by seeing you with him I'd turned away.'

'I hope the next time you see him will be in court, along with your fellow accusers.'

Kitty went very quiet. 'I completely misread the situation. No wonder Gramps told me I needed to hear your side of the story.'

'He gives wise counsel, your gramps.'

'I overreacted big time. And badly misjudged you when I should have known better. I… I think I was still in shock after the way he grabbed me and was then so vile. Can you forgive me?'

'There's absolutely nothing to forgive. He should never have been allowed in the door. Next party, we really will have security guards.'

'I've been wanting to ask you. That party. Is mixing with that kind of people what you want to do for the rest of your life? A lot of them were really boring.'

'You mean the pompous windbags?' he said.

'And the droning narcissists. The trustees of the foundation were so much nicer.'

'Agree. Hand-picked by Lady Enid and not Sir Cyril as these people were. Although they're not all bad, you must admit. Some of them were fun.'

'But is upholding the money-making stream of the Delfont family really all you want to do with your life? Your friends in the band told me you like to jam with them on trumpet and you're really talented.'

'A hobby only.' He paused. 'Before I inherited, when I had no idea I was going to end up with the title, I thought I'd like to write a novel.'

'Like your mother?'

He shook his head. 'A crime novel. A dark story with a damaged detective hero and lots of twists and turns in the plot.'

'Where revenge is delivered and justice prevails in the end?'

'Something like that. I wrote two novels, planned a series with my damaged hero.'

'What happened to them?'

'They're under the bed, never to see the light of day.'

'I'd like to read them.'

'One day, perhaps.' Or he might burn them, wipe them from his computer.

She paused. 'Talking of your mother, I'm sorry I said she'd given me unrealistic expectations about men.'

He frowned. 'Did you say that?'

'You know I did. Now I realise reading her books set me up for meeting you. Down with my gran in Widefield, I read so many of them.'

'What do you mean?' He had no idea what she was getting at.

'You're one of her honourable Spanish heroes

stepped right off the pages. It's like I was programmed to fall for you—to recognise you when I met you.'

'Isn't that a bit fanciful?' he said.

'Perhaps. It's just a strong feeling.'

'Have you fallen for me?' he said slowly.

She hesitated. 'Head over heels, just like in a Marisol Matthew novel.' She looked up at him. 'Only…only I love you in real life.'

Never had those words resonated with him so strongly. Happiness surged through him. 'I love you too, Kitty. Love at first sight, just like in one of her books. I didn't believe it could happen. But I fell for you the first day I met you. I just didn't realise because I didn't recognise what it was to fall in love.'

'Me too. Fell for you straight away. I complained to Claudia that she hadn't warned me about how hot you were. You were very distracting.'

'And you brought sunshine into what was shaping up to be a rather gloomy life.'

He cradled her face in his hand and kissed her long and slow and tenderly.

Kitty felt flooded with emotions, not the least of which was relief that the incident with Edmund Blaine had been a misunderstanding and that Sebastian had defended her and exacted revenge on the horrible man. There was joy that he had followed her down here, had gained the respect of her grandfather and had fought for her. But, most of all, there was the exquisite happiness of knowing he loved her.

She kissed him back, hoping she transmitted the joy and love she felt. This was how it was meant to be. She never wanted to be parted from him again.

She broke away from his kiss. 'We have some catching up to do,' she murmured against his mouth.

'We do,' he said. 'So much we need to tell each other.'

'That too,' she said. 'But it's not what I meant. We wasted an entire night and morning when we could have been together. That was my fault. I need to make it up to you.'

'And just how do you intend to do that?' he said, his voice husky, his eyes narrowed.

'Did you realise there's a rather wonderful bed in this room?'

'It hadn't escaped my notice,' he said.

'And the room is rather warm,' she said. 'I think we're wearing far too many clothes.'

'It is indeed heating up,' he said as he pushed her parka from her shoulders and threw it on the sofa. She kicked off her boots; he did the same with his. He started to undo the buttons on her shirt, his hands brushing against her already aroused nipples.

'My turn first,' she said, her breath coming short. She rid him of his jacket then his fine knit sweater. She slid her hands over the hard muscles of his chest, the smoothness of his olive skin, his broad shoulders, as she revelled in the sense of possession the knowledge that he loved her gave her. He was hers and she wanted to brand him with her touch.

'Strangely enough, I'm not cooling down,' he said as his hands slid inside her shirt to undo her bra.

'Me neither,' she said. 'Quite the opposite, in fact.' She gasped as he tugged off her shirt and her bra, cupping her breasts, rolling her nipples between his fingers. She could quite happily take him now, she ached for him, but she wanted to prolong the exquisite torture of desire.

She let him help her with his belt but then pushed his hand away. 'This is my pleasure,' she said.

'Mine too,' he gasped, gripping her shoulders.

She made the act of removing his trousers an extended caress, more so as she took off his boxers. She took him in her hand, admiring his strength and virility and rejoicing in the power she had to arouse him.

'No more,' he groaned. 'I want to come with you.'

Impatiently, he picked her up and carried her to the bed.

'I love it when you hold me like this,' she murmured from the security of his strong arms. 'I'm afraid I'll never be able to return the favour.'

'There are other favours you can return,' he said huskily, lying her on the bed. 'Just not right now.' He kissed her, then broke away to kiss each breast in turn, then down to the edge of her jeans. Impatient for his intimate touch, she wiggled out of her jeans, leaving her just in her pink lace panties. He pulled them off with his teeth, slid them down her thighs, then made love to her with his tongue and mouth to bring her to a climax so intense she felt light-headed.

When she'd got her breath back, she urged him towards her. 'I want you inside me, now,' she moaned.

He needed no further urging and entered her. His rhythm soon had her climbing for the peak again and she came with him, their cries of ecstasy mingling in the privacy of the room.

'You really are amazing in every way, Sir Boyfriend,' she murmured as she snuggled against him and slid into a satisfied sleep.

She woke to find Sebastian sitting on the bed next to her, dressed in the hotel's luxurious black robe, looking impossibly handsome.

'How thoughtful of the hotel to have a robe in your favourite colour,' she said as she sat up, clutching the sheet to her breasts.

He pushed the sheet away from her. 'Don't

cover yourself,' he said. 'You have no idea how lovely you look, with your hair all wild around your shoulders. I could never have enough of you.'

'You say the nicest things,' she said. And he did. He made her feel good about herself in every way. How could she have doubted him?

'I've called for lunch. It should be here soon.'

'Good,' she said.

He took her hand. 'Before it arrives, there's something I want to say to you.'

He looked into her face and she was stunned at the unmasked love that shone from his grey eyes. 'I'm asking you to marry me, Kitty. I love you and want to make you my wife.'

Kitty swallowed hard against a lump of emotion. For all her fantasies of him, she had never envisaged this moment, never dared dream that far ahead.

'Yes. I say yes to becoming your wife. I love you, Sebastian.'

He reached for the pocket of his robe, pulled out a small Tiffany blue box. 'After you agreed to come to the party on Thursday, I went shopping. I wanted to be ready. Just in case.'

Just in case he happened to propose. Wasn't that just Sebastian? How she loved him for it.

He handed the box to her. 'Before I put it on your finger, I want to make sure you like it.'

'I'll like whatever you chose,' she said.

'Just to be sure,' he said.

Of course he'd want to be absolutely sure. That was Sebastian and another of the reasons she loved him.

With fingers that weren't quite steady, she opened the box, fumbling a little with the lid. Inside was a diamond ring nestled in dark velvet, a very large classic solitaire on a fine platinum band.

'It's…it's perfect,' she said, her voice breaking. 'Simple and elegant. I love it.' She held out her left hand, fingers splayed. She couldn't help but be glad she'd had that manicure the day before.

Sebastian looked delighted as he slid the ring onto the third finger of her left hand. It fitted perfectly.

'I wanted to ask you to marry me in a more romantic location,' he said.

'What could be more romantic than this gorgeous country house hotel? It's perfect. I do have a request for our honeymoon though,' she said.

'Anywhere in the world you want,' he said.

'I'd like it to be a certain farmhouse in Mallorca,' she said. There she would find more clues to what made Sir Sebastian tick, so she could better understand him. Not to mention escaping the English weather to the milder climate of the Balearic Isles.

Her answer pleased him, she could tell.

'I promise no chickens in the kitchen,' he said.

She laughed 'Or goats in the laundry room.'

'If we're talking honeymoons already, I'd like to get married as soon as we can. I want you living with me as my wife, and mistress of the house you've helped bring to life. And perhaps wielding your PR skills for the Lady Enid foundation.'

'I'd like that very much,' she said. She and Claudia would have to sort out how her commitment to PWP would pan out; she wouldn't let her friend down. Perhaps she could still keep a stake in the business, while not actually packing boxes.

Kitty held her hand up to the light and little rainbows danced around the room. 'I absolutely love this ring.' She paused. 'Do you mind if after lunch we go back to the rehab hospital to show Gramps?'

'I was going to suggest that myself,' he said. 'Then perhaps we can have a video call with my *abuela*. She'll be very happy with our news.'

She admired the ring again, then looked back up at him. 'Does this mean I can call you Sir Fiancé?'

'Why not?' he said as he swept her into his arms.

CHAPTER SEVENTEEN

Four weeks later,
St Swithun's Church, Widefield, Kent

SEBASTIAN STOOD AT the altar of the small thirteenth-century stone church in the village where Kitty had lived with her grandparents since she was fourteen. Her grandparents had been married in this church, so had her parents; Kitty herself had been christened here. Her grandmother had done the altar flowers for many years and her grandfather still helped tend the grounds. There had been no other choice for their marriage ceremony. Sebastian appreciated the feeling of continuity and community he had been welcomed into.

At Kitty's request, the wedding was small and low-key, just family and close friends. And the staff from Cheyne Walk, of course.

It was the week before Christmas and the church was decorated with masses of magnificent blooms organised by Kitty's florist. But there was also a nativity scene set up near the sanctuary, which somehow added an extra layer of celebration. Christmas had never been a big deal for him, but Kitty loved Christmas and loved the idea that their wedding anniversary and Christmas would be so close.

Now he waited alongside the minister, flanked by his groomsmen: his two best friends from university and his favourite Spanish cousin. Kitty and her bridesmaids—Claudia and two university friends—were fashionably late by ten minutes.

In the front row sat his *abuela* and other Spanish family. His *abuela* had told him she had a feeling in her bones that this marriage would break the curse and she looked forward to many English great-grandchildren. Sebastian hadn't passed that one by Kitty yet, although they'd agreed they wanted children, sooner rather than later.

Thoughtful Kitty had set up a small table with framed photos of the people who couldn't be there to celebrate with them: her uncle and cousins in Canada, friends living in Australia and also the family who had passed away—her parents and grandmother, his parents, Uncle Olly, even Sir Cyril and Lady Enid. Somehow Kitty's beloved childhood dog, a golden Labrador named Peter, also had his photo there. Sebastian had carefully placed Peter in front of Sir Cyril, to mask his cruel face with a sweet doggy smile.

Just as he was again checking his watch, the organ struck up the wedding march. There were murmurings of anticipation among the congregation and heads turned towards the entrance of the church. Who would be the first to spot the bride?

Sebastian's heart started to thud. First the bridesmaids glided up the aisle, each in the same gown but in different pastel shades: pink, lavender and a soft blue.

Then Kitty was there, starting her journey up the aisle towards him. Surely she was the most beautiful bride ever, in a floor-length white gown with long tight lace sleeves, and little white boots peeping out from under the skirt. She wore a halo of white flowers on her head and her hair fell in soft waves around her face and over her shoulders.

Hers was a slow procession as her grandfather was still on crutches, but Kitty had insisted that no one else could be there for her and Stan had refused the option of being pushed in a wheelchair.

It was a cold, grey December day. But when Kitty and Gramps were halfway up the aisle the sun came out from behind a cloud and a shaft of sunlight shone through the ancient stained-glass window like a spotlight on Kitty, lighting her hair to a shimmering gold. The effect was so striking, everyone gasped. But Sebastian was not surprised. From the morning he had first met her, Kitty had brought sunshine to his life—and he knew she would continue to do so.

* * *

Kitty took small steps to keep up with Gramps's slow progress on crutches. She cherished every minute with her beloved grandfather. Sebastian had invited him to come and make his home with them in Cheyne Walk but Gramps was determined to stay in the village he had always loved.

As they neared the altar, Kitty looked up to see Sebastian. She didn't see the smiling faces of her family and friends, scarcely noticed the familiar beauty of the church. She only had eyes for Sebastian, his eyes full of love and anticipation and joy.

She knew they weren't supposed to kiss at the start of the ceremony, but she couldn't resist a kiss of love and affirmation on his lips when she took her place at his side, to the happy sighs of the congregation.

All too soon the timeless traditional ceremony was over, their rings had been exchanged and they had pledged their lives to each other. The minister pronounced them man and wife, Sebastian and Kitty, Sir Sebastian and Lady Kathryn Delfont. It seemed surreal that she now had a title; it would take some getting used to. But the most important title she had was *wife* to the man she loved. 'You may now kiss the bride,' the minister intoned.

Their kiss was long and heartfelt and their friends started to clap. Flushed and laughing, she broke away from the kiss. 'I suppose I can call you Sir Husband now,' she murmured.

'I like the sound of that, Lady Wife,' he said as he took her hand to walk down the aisle and celebrate their new life with the people who loved them.

* * * * *

If you enjoyed this story, check out these other great reads from Kandy Shepherd

Falling for the Secret Princess
One Night with Her Millionaire Boss
From Bridal Designer to Bride
Their Royal Baby Gift

All available now!